CHRISTOPHER J. STOCKWELL

Sleeping in the Daytime

Novella One

Editing by Nicole Fegan
Editing by Laura Stockwell
Cover art by Muhammad Maysum

This book was professionally typeset on Reedsy.
Find out more at reedsy.com

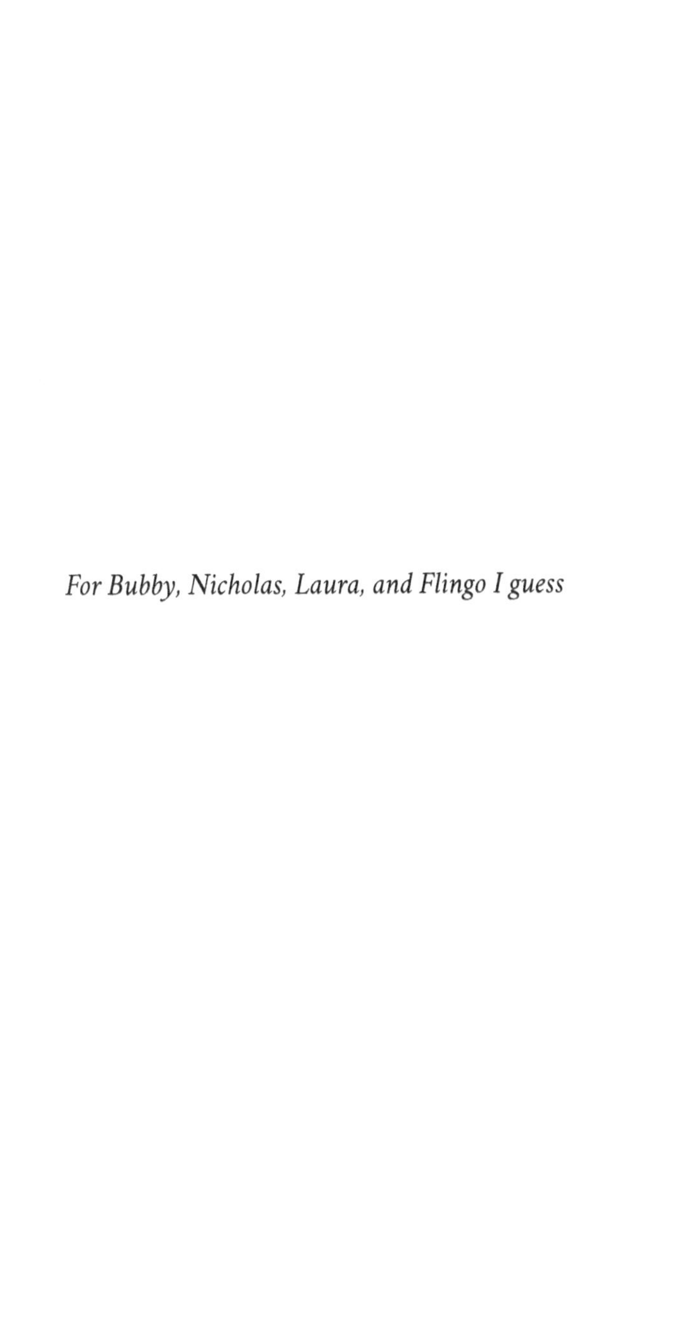

For Bubby, Nicholas, Laura, and Flingo I guess

Living like this is a full-time business.

—Irvine Welsh,
Trainspotting

Preface

"Why do you write?" She asked me during my first press interview for this book. "Why do you fuckin' care," is what my bestie Jack would say. He's always inside me trying to push his way out. When people take a tone, or give me orders, Jack bristles. Chris has a wife, kids, and a mortgage, so most of the time, Chris is charged with keeping Jack in check. Jack is why I write. The world moved on without Jack. His music scene is nothing but burnt ash from the campfire the night before. Jack's city doesn't exist anymore. It might as well be called Seattle 2.0.

I'm a lawyer, a prosecutor. When I put on a suit, you can't see me, or should I say you see my mask. Who am I? I'm the counterculture hiding in plain sight. Punk rock gave me a worldview, and I bring that worldview into society every time I speak in a courtroom or you flip the page of one of my books.

Why do I write, because after all these years, Jack and I are still pissed off at the world and everyone in it. And we've still got something to say about it.

Prologue

Was I speaking for Jack, or was Jack speaking for me? I'm the narrator, and while I do most of the speaking in this story, I never get an opportunity to really speak. Jack has got a lot to say, and most of it requires some high-brow interpretation from yours truly. The PNW hoi polloi vernacular takes a little gettin' used to, you know. Fortunately, I'm well versed. So well versed in fact, that it seems like Jack and I used to be the same person. If not the same, then nearly identical, and certainly inseparable.

At some point that changed. I'm not sure when, but it did. He went down the left fork, and I the right. Jack's story became more compelling as he became less salvageable. My story became less interesting as I became more capable. So I became the caretaker of Jack's story just as Beth became the caretaker of his mind. I hope I did it justice.

Chapter 1

Jack was addicted to everything: everything he'd ever done, everywhere he'd ever been, and everyone he'd ever met. Painful, pleasurable—it didn't matter; he'd been addicted to it. The only thing he'd never been addicted to was a peaceful, simple life. That life never presented itself to him, but if it had, he might have become addicted to it, too. Probably not, but maybe. Sometimes he had used to wonder about that. Jack had used to daydream that if the sweet plainness of a domestic life ever became a reality for him, it would be the last addiction he'd ever need. That seemed far-fetched, but it gave him something to wonder about.

Jack had never really had a chance. In fact, Jack's *generation* had never really had a chance. He was a microcosm of Generation X and, as such, a perfect representative of the gritty little group. Gen X was like the sinking of the *Titanic*. A whole bunch of people died miserably under terrifying circumstances and for no good reason at all. All of the survivors were traumatized for life, and they lived the remainder of their lives miserable and terrified. They wound up broken toys, shoved in a corner that the world never managed to dispose of. That was Gen X, broken toys occupying space.

There is no happy ending for Jack, but there is a story, and it's a story worth telling. After all, there weren't that many Gen Xers in the first place, there are a lot less of them now, and even fewer of them that would bother to tell the story of a guy like Jack.

Chapter 2

J ack was twenty-eight and was once again inside an institution. Fairfax Psychiatric Hospital, this time. This was actually his second time at Fairfax, but it wouldn't have mattered if it was his first or his fiftieth. It was nothing new to Jack. He'd lived in more institutions in his lifetime than actual residences.

Institutions were his homes, and he'd always felt comfortable in them. That might have been because they always looked the same. The nasty ones had pink tiles in the bathrooms and disgusting ammonia-soaked linoleum on the floor. The smell was always the same, too. Not only did the ammonia fail to cover up the smell, which could only be described as human desperation, but it was actually an integral part of the aroma. The nice ones were simply well-kept wings of nicer hospitals. Jack typically ended up in the nasty ones.

Despite a hundred diagnoses from a hundred different psychiatrists, nobody really knew what was wrong with Jack's brain. Bipolar disorder, obsessive-compulsive disorder, borderline schizophrenia, depression, panic disorder, and post-traumatic stress disorder were some of the most commonly recurring diagnoses. Any or all of those diagnoses could have been accurate. It was safe to say that at least one or more were. What was undisputed was that, on top of whatever else was going on with Jack, he was a bona fide alcoholic, straddling the knife's edge of addiction with every other substance he had ever tried.

At that time, Jack was still in denial. Jack wasn't crazy—not according to Jack. Of course, the more time he spent in places like Fairfax, the crazier he felt. As of that day, he still considered himself a tourist. No, not a tourist; more like a distant relative who was visiting. Jack fit because he had just a touch of mental illness, but those other people were the really crazy ones. He had just flown in for the holidays, and then he'd be back to his glamorous life in the outside world.

Chapter 3

J ack's final meeting with the Fairfax staff psychiatrist went well. In his time, he'd had many final meetings with psychiatrists. To Jack, they were simply a matter of giving canned answers to canned questions. What was his concrete plan for reintegrating into society? Where would he be staying? Was his SSI, GAU, or whatever government program he'd be drawing funds from, in order? Did he have phone numbers for potential therapists? Had his court-appointed social workers set up other services for him? Jack knew what to say to get released: yes, to all of the above.

And not just yes to all: Jack had a song and dance about his plan to join the workforce of this great nation after the successful completion of whatever three-to-six-month vocational program he was pretending to be interested in, and that he was going over to such and such trade school first thing Monday morning to fill out an application for such and such vocational program. Everybody won:

the psychiatrist got to sign off on a successful release and rehabilitation of a malfunctioning societal cog, and Jack got to return to the dull roar of insanity he enjoyed when he was out. Most importantly, he got another crack at making it in the normal world.

Really, though, living on the outside never lasted long for Jack. Despite his honest desire to make it work on the outside, he always wound up behind locked doors sooner rather than later. Jack prided himself on being an intellectual loser. He read books that made him appear smart and quoted only the most obvious and memorable portions of the philosophy books he sort of read. At that time Jack's pseudo-intellectual observation was that most people lived their lives behind locked doors, and in that way, Jack reasoned, he wasn't so different from them. Their locked doors were the ones inside of their own brains. Everyone that had ever walked the earth, he pontificated, was behind a locked door of some sort. The sad thing was, they didn't even know it. Normal people had internalized the caged mentality. Normal people, he reasoned, didn't need physical cages anymore. They needed to own things to have security. They needed to make house payments, car payments, and payments into their retirement funds so they could move somewhere warm when they retired. They were imprisoned by their own perceived needs.

Jack's pontifications became more and more elaborate. He imagined that some people knew the truth about the state of things and spent their entire lives rebelling against it. They preached their revolutionary rhetoric to anyone who would listen. In that way, they became slaves of their own ideological angst. None of that changed the fact that Jack always ended up behind an actual, physical locked door. It was a clever false equivalency that allowed Jack to see himself as the same or better than everyone else, but, secretly, he imagined that those metaphorical cages might be the way to go.

Jack admired his father and brother, their gritty tenacity. They knew the world was out to grind them under its heel, and they would always just grind right back. They simply accepted that life was about pain and suffering, and that small glimpses of happiness were all most people ever got. Those types were mostly free. Mostly.

Jack knew all these things but lacked the backbone to do things for the right reasons, or even out of a feeling of responsibility to the people he cared about, or who cared about him. He was a disgusting example of excess, self-centeredness, and a general lack of ability to deal. He used substances, sex, gambling, and anything else he could put his hands on to make his way through the world. That's where Jack fit in. Jack was imprisoned by everything, especially his addictions, because of a helpless inability to meet the world on the world's terms. Jack didn't accept the world, his place in it, or his defective brain, and Jack wasn't free.

Jack's first morning out of Fairfax was actually going pretty well. This time he'd been in for almost a year. A long stay by his standards, but he'd been in fairly rough shape when they'd committed him. Jack's mom had just died, and the remainder of anything that resembled a support system along with her. Jack's father had died a few years before, but that hadn't affected him the same way. His father hadn't offered much in the way of emotional support. It had bothered Jack's father to have a son that, in his mind, refused to toughen up and make his own way in life like he and Jack's big brother Laurence had. Jack was a momma's boy. Jack's mom was the only person who saw more than a lazy, freeloading loser when she looked at him.

After Jack's mom died, things were different for him. When she died, he knew his days were numbered, as his ability to survive had always depended on his mom's support. After she was gone, there was no one to bail Jack out anymore. Jack was really on his own. Jack's mom had been saving his life at least once a year since kindergarten. "Now who'd save me?" Jack wondered. "How would I make it through even one year on my own?" Those had been the thoughts running through his head at his mom's funeral, and Jack was ashamed those had been his thoughts at that moment. While others had wept at the loss of this loving, caring woman, Jack had shaken with fear at the prospect of his own impending doom. After the funeral, it had been all of six days before Jack was committed to Fairfax. Unlike most of Jack's trips, that time, Jack had been in no hurry to leave. "There was nowhere for me to go that time, but after nearly a year inside there, I felt like I was ready to give it a try anyway."

Jack's first stop of the morning after leaving Fairfax was the bank, where he meant to cash his SSI check. His check was wet when he handed it to the bank teller. It was November in the Puget Sound, and the "dark wet" was in full swing. His new residence should have been his first stop, but he was in no hurry to go there. When your new place was a halfway house in downtown Tacoma, you were never in a hurry to get there. The euphoric effect of the medication Jack had been prescribed at the pharmacy before his departure from Fairfax was not enough to get him to walk through the door of that halfway house. Alcohol was a necessary agent to appropriately humble him for that event.

Yes, things were definitely different that time for Jack. No car, no mom, no prospects. That was exactly where Jack's little story should have turned around or ended. It did neither. If Jack had been the protagonist of a feel-good movie, he would have pulled himself up through therapy, tenacity, and hard work. He would have met a girl, found meaning in his existence, and gone antiquing on Sundays. It would be a short movie. But Jack wasn't a simple guy, and his story was complicated. There was a girl, though. There were actually quite a few—and one in particular—but that one definitely wasn't Lisa.

Lisa's place was always a good spot for Jack to crash for a few months while he was in between places. Lisa was also a good one to call up when Jack got off the bus at The Tipperary Tavern, cash from his SSI check in hand. Lisa's bed was also a good place to land when he was in between girls.

Lisa lived right up the street and was also on SSI. Somehow, she managed to keep her rent paid on the small amount of money SSI paid, something Jack had never gotten the hang of. Somehow, she also managed to only ever get high and drunk when it was on somebody else's coin. Another useful skill Jack had never gotten the hang of. After nearly a year in Fairfax Psychiatric Hospital, sex with institutionalized females had worn thin for Jack. Lisa was mentally ill, but not institutionalized. Plus, she was the only date Jack could afford on an SSI check. In days gone by, Jack's release would have been followed by a big welcome home dinner, and his mom would have slipped him the six or seven hundred bucks she'd been saving up for him. After dinner with his mom, it would have been booze, drugs, and whores for however long his mom's cash had held out. This was in stark contrast to Jack's meager little celebration that day. Over five pitchers of Rainier (two of which Lisa finished by herself despite being half Jack's size), Jack wondered if there was cause for celebration at all.

Humping Lisa was neither exciting nor new, but after they staggered out of the Tipperary to her place, Jack did it anyway. Somehow, Jack purposely missed the eight o'clock curfew at the halfway house. He would therefore have to stay the night at Lisa's. Jack didn't mind. He knew what he was doing, and it already had him concerned, but not concerned enough to make curfew. Where was his resolve, his concrete plan to reintegrate? It was gone, just like his SSI money would be if he stayed at Lisa's for much longer. Actually, that was not the truth at all; his resolve had never really been there, and he knew it. His SSI money evaporating over pitchers with Lisa at the Tipperary would be the truth if he stuck around there much longer, though.

His head felt clear again. It was past ten at night and he'd been passed out for most of the day. Lisa was still out, and she would stay that way all night.

Jack's new plan was to watch some TV, try to get a few more hours of sleep, and wake up early.

For maybe the first time in his life, Jack woke up and did what he'd set out to do in the first place. It was just after six in the morning. Before he took off, he left his open pack of smokes on Lisa's nightstand. Lisa never had her own smokes. Lisa never had her own anything, and in Jack's estimation, the smokes and pitchers were payment in full for the night's lodging. He laughed a little. At least she'd have something to be happy about when she finally rolled out of bed.

Jack had spent many a night there and many times had noticed a funny thing about Lisa. She was pretty in a conventional sort of way, and also crazy in a conventional sort of way. Most people looked peaceful when they were sleeping, even crazy people. And, of course, Jack had seen his share of crazy people sleeping. But Lisa never looked peaceful when she was sleeping. Lisa still looked crazy, in her conventionally crazy sort of way. When she woke up, she wouldn't wonder where Jack was, or why he hadn't said goodbye. She'd just answer the phone again in a couple of years when Jack called from the Tipperary at eleven thirty some morning.

Chapter 4

J ack finally had a chance to get into the bathroom at the halfway house. Jack's image in the mirror alarmed him. His poor appearance triggered an anxious twinge in his stomach and heart palpitations in his chest. "I've got ingrown toenails, and psoriasis on my arm, and I'm an insomniac, and I think I got athlete's foot from the showers at Fairfax," he mused. All of that existed on top of his abnormally patchy beard line, slightly receding hairline, and physique that only looked good as long as he was fully clothed.

This sort of anxiety attack was exactly the type that had historically put Jack into a downward spiral about any or all of the conditions he'd come to believe he suffered from. Right then, he became obsessed with a patch of dry skin on his right forearm, and before five minutes had elapsed, he had convinced himself that the dry skin was the beginning of flesh-eating bacteria. He erroneously reasoned that, since he'd shot heroin in that arm about two years before, he must have flesh-eating bacteria. With that, Jack was out the door to the main branch library downtown to research flesh-eating bacteria.

By that time, Jack was certainly living small. Making it to the halfway house with most of his SSI money in his pocket was a huge accomplishment for him. For Jack, an even larger accomplishment was that he was still on his meds. The application for Section Eight housing that Jack had filled out in the hospital, his state-issued identification card, and seventy-five dollars were all he needed to check into the halfway house. Seventy-five a month got you one shared 12x20 room, only slightly larger than a prison cell, but the precise dimensions of Jack's old room at Fairfax. From outside, his room there actually looked like a hospital room, but once Jack was inside, it felt like another prison cell.

The halfway house was one step above a shelter and two steps below the worst public housing. "Oh yeah, public housin', I had to go down to that fuckin' nasty-ass welfare office up on 19th and Sprague that day and check on my Section Eight application." Jack had surmised that it usually took a few months to get approved for assisted housing, but he'd gotten his application going almost two months ago while he had still been in Fairfax. In Jack's mind, that meant that he could be out of the halfway house in as little as a few weeks.

One dingy main hallway linked everything in the halfway house. At one end was the check-in desk, with an office behind it. At the other end was an outdoor, fenced-off smoking area. If a resident checked out after eight in the evening, they were out until the next morning. If a resident showed up to check in after eight, they were out until the next morning. That was a lesson Jack had learned the hard way. "Five after eight isn't before eight. For that matter, one minute before eight isn't before eight, either. As far as that goes, just because my watch says it's seven fifty-five doesn't make it before eight, either." The only clock that mattered for purposes of checkin in or out was the one on the wall behind the desk. "And if you ain't signed in by before eight, accordin' to that clock, you might as well not bother showin' up at all."

In between the front desk and smoking area were all the residents' rooms. They lined both sides of the hallway like a cellblock. Other than the rooms, there was a kitchen, a small game room, and one large bathroom that housed all the showers in that depressing all-male facility. After a couple of weeks, Jack had the place figured out. To Jack, it was a joke. He'd always show up to check in for the night, and when he wanted to go to a party, or the bar, or whatever, he just hopped the fence in the smoking area. The front door was locked after eight and attended by an employee, and the windows in the rooms didn't open at all, but the smoking area door was open all day and night. Jack always signed in before he snuck out. Once he was used to the routine, the halfway house wasn't so bad for him. Because he was able to sneak out almost every night, he even managed to reconnect with his normal party crowd. Better still, all the good drugs and downtown bars were at most a ten or fifteen-minute walk from the halfway house.

Walter never snuck out, and he was always in his bunk before ten. He woke up at six in the morning, when the morning employees came knocking on the residents' doors, and he was always out before eight in the morning, the time when they kicked the residents out for the day. Actually, he woke up half a dozen times before six, but that was just so that he could scream himself awake from his PTSD-induced Vietnam nightmares. Six was when he got his day started.

Walter was Jack's roommate at the halfway house. They didn't choose to be stuck together, and they had very little in common. They both smoked cigarettes, and Walter never had any, so they both liked Jack's cigarettes. They had that in common. Walter was so far out there that Jack wasn't really sure who Walter even was. He was a six-foot-four-inch-tall Native American man with full head of waist-length black hair. Walter's perfect hairline made Jack feel self-conscious about his own mildly receding hairline.

Walter was a Vietnam vet and had become so schizophrenic that any real living person was always the third person in a conversation with him. Eventually, Walter would get around to revealing his entire life story, but he wouldn't tell it to you. He'd tell it to the people that weren't there, and he didn't tell it like he was telling a story. It was more like he was debating whether his past had actually happened with an unseen adversary. "'NO, NO, NO, DON'T FUCKING SHOOT HER! NO!' 'GET ON THE CHOPPER WALTER! GET ON THE FUCKING CHOPPER PRIVATE!' 'FUCK YOU! THIS ISN'T REAL! THIS DIDN'T HAPPPEN! I WASN'T HERE!' "It was all fuckin' night long with Walter's night terrors and screaming, but he always narrated both parts of the conversation, so at least you could follow the story."

Walter never showered, and he smelled like it. In the six weeks Jack had spent there, he had seen Walter shower once, and then only because the halfway house employees threatened to drag him into the shower by force if he wouldn't go willingly. In a place with forty residents and five shower stalls, all of which were located next to each other, and fixed windows of time in which to bathe, everyone knew who didn't shower, and Walter didn't shower.

The reality was that Walter shouldn't have been in the halfway house at all. He should have been committed, and he had been several times. But at the end of the twentieth century in America, if you were like Walter, you fell through the cracks. Walter slept in a cot not six feet from Jack's, but that didn't bother him. The fact that Walter's attire looked like the free clothes bin at the homeless shelter had thrown up on him didn't bother Jack either. Jack single-handedly supporting Walter's smoking habit didn't even really bother him. Buying Walter like sixty cans of Coca Cola from the soda machine in the lobby was fine by Jack, too. What bothered Jack was Walter's fairly normal past, his fucked-up present, and his bleak future.

Like most roommates, Jack and Walter eventually learned to tolerate each other, even like each other. Or, more accurately, Jack learned how to tolerate Walter. Walter seemed to like Jack from the beginning, and Jack suspected that Walter would have liked anyone who tolerated bunking with him. Despite that, Walter's mere existence bothered Jack. This scared Jack like nothing else ever had. Walter had graduated from high school. Walter had been to war overseas. Walter had been married, had children, even had a decent job for many years. All the while, he had been fighting his schizophrenia. For much of his life, Walter had been relatively successful for someone struggling with extreme mental illness. In fact, Walter had held his life together for over thirty years before completely deteriorating.

Jack had never been successful or stable, and he was pushing thirty right then. If this was where Walter, who'd managed an essentially normal life for so many years, had ended up, where would Jack, who had never managed to disguise or disregard his neuroses, find himself? Even if Jack knew he would eventually end up like Walter, he preferred to avoid staring it in the face, and bunking with Walter was staring it in the face every day.

Chapter 5

For Jack, kissing the foul stench of the halfway house goodbye was cause for celebration. Saying hello to the foul stench of his new place was also cause for celebration. Jack scratched his head: dandruff. Jack scratched his eyebrow: dandruff. Even though he had severe dandruff on both his scalp and in his eyebrows, he still felt a cut above the other residents at his new building. Jack caught a glance of his slightly receding hairline in an outside building window at that time of the day when the window was basically a mirror. "Hopefully," he thought, "if my hairline recedes any more, the dandruff will disappear with the hair." However, a bald man whose dandruff persisted despite his lack of hair would fit in perfectly at Jack's new building.

Who else fit in there? The young black woman that had severe brain damage from a catastrophic car accident who used a walker and sat in the foyer all day bumming cigarettes? She fit in. The sweaty, longhaired butt-rocker with the gigantic plasma donation scars on both arms? He fit in, too. All the old people that had no families to take care of them but were not ready for the nursing home? You bet they fit in. The guy with one arm? Oh yeah, that guy definitely fit in. The HIV positive gay dudes that fucked anything they could get their hands on when they were well enough to get out of bed? You had better believe they fit in. How about the screwball alcoholic building management team? Anybody that would work there clearly couldn't get a job anywhere better, so yeah, they fit just like recycled condoms: wet and loose. Everybody there belonged, Jack thought, except him. Whether they were on the last stop of a long, underprivileged life, or just layovers on short, miserable ones, everybody there belonged, and if they didn't when they arrived, they would within a few years. Or, as Jack always said, "You can only slum it there for a while before you become a permanent fixture."

Here, was The Winthrop Apartments. It was one of the most interesting buildings in Tacoma. The Winthrop Apartments were constructed in the twenties as the swanky, high-end Winthrop Hotel. The time period in which they were constructed was made evident by its enormous closets and tiny bathrooms. People used to travel with baggage, lots of baggage.

Before there were transatlantic flights two thousand times a day, traveling could be arduous and time consuming. Just the travel time involved in most early twentieth century long-distance journeys was equivalent or greater to entire vacations these days. Back then, you'd spend a week on a ship crossing the Atlantic or on a train crossing the continent. Today, people started their vacations by getting on the red-eye at two in the morning on a Monday, and they were back on the same flight heading home the following week so that they could be at work Monday morning, not a very relaxing vacation.

Those travelers from the early twentieth century measured their trips in months, sometimes years, never weeks or days. If you were leaving home for months or years, closet space was preferable to bathroom space, or even sleeping space, for that matter. The building's tenure as the grand lodging of the south sound, however, was short-lived. Tacoma was not much of a tourist attraction, and from the environs, one supposed it never really was.

The Winthrop fell into disrepair almost immediately. It was sold a few times before the Conifer group bought it in the seventies. Finally, someone had found the building's market niche. Over two hundred units in a building with no grounds, or parking, best of all very little upkeep. They realized that the units were not adequate for apartments, not without major remodeling, which would have cut the number of units in half. Nor was the building any longer adequate as a hotel. But as low-income apartments, it was a cash cow.

Poor people on public housing, such as the residents of the Winthrop, didn't expect prompt repair of problems in their apartments, and even if they did, what could they do if they didn't get them? If they were in subsidized housing—and all the residents were—it took months to find another place, so they'd just deal with the habitation issues. For the owners, converting to low-income housing meant they got full market value for each subpar unit. Housing and Urban Development paid the owners the difference for what they didn't receive directly from their tenants. Better yet, there was a steady stream of subsidized housing applicants in Tacoma, so the apartments were always full. The Conifer Group got the full market value for each unit every month and barely put a dime back in for maintenance.

"Sometimes, when I close my eyes, I can read these things, ya know. Like, the things I can read behind my eyes always seem important, or like they should be important to someone, just not important to me. And they're very detailed. Behind my eyes none of it reads simple, though. Detailed directions for building all sorts of things pop into my head.

I always see these entire poems, or chapters from what I figure are classic books of literature that I've never read. Sometimes, I can read the entire script to an episode of a television show that won't air till next season. Then I fuckin' see it the next season, and I'm like WTF!

"When this shit comes, I can read as quickly or slowly as I like. I can try to comprehend as much or as little as I like. But once I've moved on to the next line of text, the previous line disappears into the space above. Like at the beginning of *Star Wars*. I guess there's only so much room on the movie screen of my brain. It's free information, information that I'm not bright enough to put to good use, or maybe I just don't understand its significance yet.

"Maybe, just maybe, it's shit I was never meant to receive. Like somethin' got some wires crossed somewhere, and now I can eavesdrop on sensitive material that was en route to someone important. I'm spliced in on some celestial phone line that runs over my apartment on the way to a spiritual or world leader somewhere. Sometimes, when I pick up that phone, I get some fuzz, static backwash, not enough to do any damage with. Maybe someday I'll get somethin' really sensitive, somethin' I can use to extort some rich fucker or the government into givin' me millions of dollars. That'd be fuckin' kewl!"

Jack knew somewhere in the city there was an apartment building with normal people, with normal lives, that he could get into with his HUD application. There were these sorts of mixed, or subsidized and unsubsidized, apartment complexes all over the city. You just had to look for them. Getting into one took a while, but it was a real option for someone like Jack. "Why didn't I never have no premonition tellin' me where to find those elusive buildins'?" The reality was that he had never looked. If he was being honest with himself, he knew that living somewhere with a bunch of normal apartment dwellers wasn't for him. Instead, he chose to live in a studio apartment that was the size of a closet, with a closet that was big enough to fit a bathtub inside, and a bathroom that was too small for the toilet and bathtub that were already in it. It was no wonder the residents in that place were crazy. Just negotiating the dimensions of those units could drive a sane person mad.

Then, of course, there were the roaches, and then there were more roaches, and then there were a few hundred thousand roaches after that. Jack was too tired, though. He didn't even mind the roaches so much, so as long as they stayed out of his sleeping space. They never did. Sometimes, when the lamp Jack had found on the street was on and he was lying on the pee-soaked mattress he had found next to the lamp, he could see them running up and down the walls. Sometimes, they ran across the ceiling, down the TV screen, up the sink drain, and anywhere else they saw fit to run.

During that time, it seemed that Jack had fallen into the trap that many people with little to do fell into. Sleep. "Sleep was my master." When he lived in the halfway house, he knew he had to be out at a certain time, and that sleeping was only allowed during certain hours. At the institution, he had a structured existence as well. Not that the residents at either place did anything important with their time. But the structure was there. Now, Jack had a steady SSI check and a closet-sized apartment with its bedroom-sized closet. Sleep could be done at any point in the day. Any hour was his to sleep, and he slept whenever he didn't feel like sitting upright. The less you had to do, the more you slept. Ask any convict. Jack's idea of paradise became a big comfortable bed with clean sheets. This was also how Jack envisioned heaven, but in heaven the sheets were designer and silk. "Yep, that's right, I saw it in a vision one time."

When getting a comfortable bed so that you could forget your waking hours in style became important, you were done for. You were really done, you had lost, life had beat you like an abused dog, and that bed was just a placeholder for the coffin that would shortly replace it. Jack took too much solace in the fact that he still found the energy to get up to urinate in the toilet instead of his bed. There were times when Jack considered adding a few of his own pee stains to the preexisting ones. "Thus far, I hadn't, but I've been tempted. Other of my bodily fluids that exit the body through the penis had found their way onto that mattress, though." However, not nearly as much of them as one might think. Most of the time, knocking back off for a few hours seemed more interesting to Jack than jerking off. Jack had a new addiction: sleep.

He wasn't drinking. He wasn't gambling. He wasn't doping. He wasn't popping pills. He wasn't soliciting prostitutes. He also wasn't living. Over the past several weeks, his waking time had dwindled down to about eight hours a day. The average workday of a normal person was now the lump sum of consciousness for Jack's entire day.

During the rare interludes where Jack was conscious, he thought life on the third floor was somewhat nice most of the time. The two ground floors were not numbered, so the third floor was more like the fifth floor, but in the elevator, the button you pushed to get to Jack's place was three.

On the third floor that was actually the fifth floor, Jack was high enough up that the street noise didn't really bother him, but low enough so that he wasn't constantly tempted to take that liberating leap out his window into eternal freedom. From that height, it was just too risky. Jack imagined that, from that height, he was more likely to wind up bouncing off the hood of a car and living the rest of his miserable existence in a wheelchair, unable to even make another jumping attempt.

From the eighth, ninth, or tenth floors, death was pretty much assured. "How do those fuckin' people live up there?" Jack wondered. Jack could ride the elevator up to the tenth floor, walk right out onto the fenced observation area of the roof, hop over the three-foot tall chain link fence, stroll out to the edge, and swan dive for all of downtown to see. At any point, he could do it, and he'd walked to the elevator for that purpose several times, but it took five minutes for the elevator just to get to his floor. By the time the elevator actually got there, some drunk had always stumbled by, or a blue-haired geriatric, buzzed up on her medication rambled by. That was when Jack would always tell himself that if they weren't jumping that day, neither would he. Then, he'd turn around and walk back to his closet apartment and take a nap.

Chapter 6

For a few hours, Jack forgot about Walter at the halfway house. He forgot about the impending doom his mental deterioration would inevitably bring him in the future. For a little while, he didn't even mind his third-floor, closet-sized apartment. For a few hours, he sunk into a shameless remembrance of his days as a juvenile delinquent, all because of a lucky find in the garbage that morning.

It was 1985 again. Jack saw Black Flag at the Community World Theater. BO-soaked leather jackets, second-hand smoke from generic brand cigarettes, and that tangy aluminum smell of cheap beer in a can were the holy trinity of aromas for the punk scene. If punk had a cologne, that was it. He'd been going to punk shows for a couple of years, but most of what he was interested in were local bands like the Fartz or the Wipers. Black Flag was from LA, and they were playing in Tacoma for a crowd of seventy or eighty. Even with the sparse crowd, the room was elbow to elbow. Ninety percent of the hall was completely vacant, all but a piece of floor no larger than 20x20 feet. Every person who was not working the door, selling merchandise at the table in the back, operating the sound board, or performing on stage was squeezed into the tiny plot of land in front of the stage.

Between a fairly significant concussion and his normal alcohol-induced blackout, Jack didn't remember much of the show, but he remembered them playing a song called "Depression." He'd heard it before. He'd heard all their songs before. He had spent the last year listening to all their seven inches, and the last week listening to nothing but Black Flag in anticipation of that Tacoma show. Still, the "Depression" lyrics rang like church bells in his head. They rang so hard it seemed like they rang backwards in time so that, afterward, he could always hear them overlaid on memories of his early childhood. They rang into the future, too. After that night, they were always imprinted somewhere transparent, baked into every experience from then on. Jack thought he'd probably taken some acid that night after he was wasted. He couldn't remember for sure. The acid wore off, but those lyrics ringing in his brain like some time-travelling bell never really stopped. Sometimes they got a little quieter, but that song told him a truth about himself, and he could never unring that bell.

Before that, the Crescent Ballroom was the only place worth putting on an all-ages punk show in Tacoma. A couple of years later, the Community World Theater in south Tacoma would have a short but illustrious career as the punk venue of choice. A very forgettable band named Nirvana played their very first show there, and at the time Jack had assumed it would be their last. A year or two after that, the Crescent Ballroom would become Legends. In the early nineties, there was a place in the basement of a Stihl Chainsaw store called, somewhat unoriginally, The Chainsaw, where several people were nearly killed during an Accused show, which was, notably, the most violent room Jack had ever stepped into, then or now. There were a lot of other venues; most existed for a matter of months, sometimes weeks, but those three or four were on his mind that afternoon.

On a normal day back then, Jack would wake up late, skip school, skate, get stoned, skate, get stoned again, get drunk, masturbate, and pass out. Next day, repeat. And so on and so forth. Sometimes he'd even squeeze a meal in, but whatever was going on, the punk rock soundtrack blared in the background like war drums. Jack was so baked right then that he faded out of consciousness as the Shit Split spun away on his new record player.

Jack's new place was right across the hall from the third-floor garbage room, which had some definite advantages and more than its share of disadvantages. Most of what Jack currently owned came from the garbage room. There was no garbage chute in that building, just a room with galvanized-steel garbage cans. Every floor had a room like that one across from Jack's apartment, and living across from the one on his floor gave Jack the bug, the garbage-digging bug. All he had needed was a taste, and he was hooked.

For once in his life, Jack seemed to have acquired a habit that wasn't harmful to anyone, including himself. One of his few daily activities had become ransacking the garbage rooms of each and every floor in the building. It was tricky; even in a building with only a couple hundred tenants, Jack immediately realized that the competition for the good garbage was fierce.

There was always new garbage because somebody was always moving, getting evicted, or dying. Not surprisingly, the departing tenants routinely left most of their meager possessions behind. Each tenant of the building was an opportunity-motivated dumpster diver. Those dilettantes put no more effort into the practice than simply grabbing anything that looked good when they were dropping off their own garbage. There were also two guys that routinely dumpster-dived the cans. Neither of them went out every day, and neither of them hit all the cans like Jack did. One hit the low floors and the other hit the higher floors. Of course, Jack hit them all, and often.

Those two guys tried a few times to ward Jack off from hitting their cans, but Jack had long ago developed his universal response to all requests from other people he didn't care for. "Get the fuck out my face" was his standard response, and more than that the ever-present mantra of Jack's life. As usual, it worked well enough to spook the dumpster divers in his building. Those two never directly confronted him after receiving the standard response, but they did start going out earlier in the day to get to the good stuff before Jack.

That day Jack hit pay dirt. It was just what he'd been looking for. An old Sanyo stereo with a turntable on it. One look verified that the needle was still attached to it. Jack's rounds for the day were over right then. He knew those other dumpster divers would get some good stuff out of the garbage he missed that day, but he didn't care, because he'd found the jewel. As soon as Jack got back to his place, he plugged in the stereo and checked out the speaker connections. The connectors on the big house speakers he'd found a couple weeks before didn't match the Sanyo, so he just chopped the connectors off the speakers' cables and wired them straight to the back of the Sanyo.

Jack's friend Todd had been babysitting his record collection. Todd was one of the only friends Jack had left. More than that, Jack actually cared about his friendship with Todd. And, even more important than that, Todd had the only possessions that Jack really cared about, Jack's records. Once Jack was confident that the Sanyo was in good working order, he immediately headed downstairs and caught the bus to Todd's.

The back door of Jack's building opened up onto a patch of sidewalk with an rusty-iron pole sticking out of it and a small, covered bus stop with a sign that had the number twenty-five on it. The iron pole stuck up about a foot out of the concrete, and it was jagged all around. Every time Jack walked out the back door, he seriously considered "accidentally" slipping and landing right on top of that jagged pole. He knew this guy who had done just that a couple of years ago on a similar hazard the city had failed to take care of, and he got six thousand dollars for what amounted to a bad cut on his butt. "Six-grand for throwin' yourself butt-first onto a pole, that was good fuckin' scratch!"

Normally, Jack was just walking out this door, headed to wherever on foot, but that day he had to sit and wait on the bus for several minutes, which gave him quite a while to ponder the iron pole. Jack's best guess was that the pole had used to be the bus stop, and that some incompetent or lazy city employee had seen the pole was cemented into the sidewalk when they built a new bus stop sign, so he had just sawed it off. "But the dumbfuck sawed it too far off the ground so any fuckin' body could just come along and plop themselves right down onto the fucker." The city never bothered to come grind it down. It was rusted to a dark red color all over, and Jack guessed it had been like that for years. He decided to reserve "accidentally" slipping on the pole as a plan b if he ever needed it. "Cause, you know, if you got evicted or somethin', six grand would be a lot more useful than it is when you already got a place to live."

The twenty-five bus took Jack almost right to Todd's door. He lived right off of Sixth Avenue, about a mile and a half away from Jack's place downtown. Jack could have walked to it in about twenty minutes, but it was raining. That was no real excuse, since it was always raining, but Jack was also characteristically lazy that day. Jack justified spending the sixty-five cents for bus fare by telling himself that the twenty-five's bus stop was right outside his back door, and it would let him off a half block from Todd's house. In this case, it was almost like Jack wasn't going outside at all. Jack hated going outside. That had to be worth spending sixty-five cents and enduring the bus people he tried so hard to avoid. Jack also hated the bus, and he was annoyed that he had to ride a thing he hated to avoid going outside. At the end of the day, Jack hated going outside more than he hated the bus. Back when he had gotten his first car, he had sworn to himself that he'd never again become so familiar with the buses that he knew which bus numbers went where, but there he was, and he knew the twenty-five went to Todd's house.

Todd was a member of the old crew. If he had a role, it would be the archivist. Unfortunately for him, he was the archivist of people and times that lacked any significance to anyone outside a handful of losers. He had artifacts from their youth that every other member of their crew had long since abandoned. His house was a museum, the sole purpose of which was to document their youth. It helped that Todd was also sort of a hoarder. If you couldn't remember the date of a show, Todd knew. He had a ticket stub, or a flyer, or a weekly paper from that week. He owned t-shirts that didn't even fit him, that had never fit him, that he got from friends in trades for no better reason than to stick it in a closet and preserve it for posterity.

Todd was tall and sort of large around the center. In fact, he was sort of large everywhere, and a little unkempt—a lot unkempt. He looked like a hibernating bear would look if you stuck a smoldering cigarette in its mouth and dressed it up in worn-out Levi's and a holey Anti-Nowhere League t-shirt. Actually, he looked more like a bear that had just woken up from hibernating, because although Todd was always awake, he never seemed all the way awake.

There were picture albums full of people Jack had forgotten even existed, people they'd met at a party, or show, and never seen again. One time, he found a letter from one of Jack's ex-girlfriends addressed to him in Todd's kitchen drawer. It was a letter Jack remembered reading, and had probably discarded in Todd's garbage, where Todd no doubt flagged it as something important and preserved it. Or it may have been in some box destined for the garbage one of the times Todd had helped Jack move. Maybe Todd had thought Jack would want it at some point in the future, or maybe he just didn't have much to remember Mandy by. As far as ex-girlfriends went, Mandy was alright, but Todd and her had hung out a lot back then. Just another example of the odds and ends one would find at Todd's house.

Todd and Jack were half of the old crew. People hear crew and think gang, but a crew was not a gang. Gangs were together for protection. Right at their cores, that was what gangs were; that was why they started, and in the end, it was all they had in common. They may pull some jobs, bury a few members, and sell mountains of dope together, but in the end, fear was all that kept them together. A gang could go on and on with new members to replace the dead or incarcerated ones. They routinely went on until no original members even existed, or even to the point where no current members knew who any of the original members even were. In a gang you were disposable, and the ranks needed to stay filled. On a block with a gang, kids were scared to not join, and once they were in, they were certainly too scared to leave.

About the only thing a gang had in common with a crew was that, in both cases, you were in for life. But that was where all similarity ended. Gangs had names, and real crews rarely ever did. You weren't beat into a crew or tattooed with the ritual gang logo. "I met guys at McNeil that had been in so many gangs they had gang tattoos coverin' up older gang tattoos. They'd just simply run out of skin."

A crew was all about love, not fear. Nobody was controlled, and nobody had anything to fear from anyone in their crew. Any real crew only lasted until the second to last member died. There were no replacements members. At some point, everybody involved knew what it was, and who was part of it. That was the moment when it became a crew and the members were linked forever.

When somebody died, the group's number dropped by one, and they were never replaced. Those tragedies were often the things that brought them back together after spanning out into the world of adult life. The strain actually revealed how strong the bonds were, not how much separation had deteriorated them.

It was not something that was put together; it grew together organically, and you couldn't manufacture one intentionally even if you wanted to. Before he was twenty-eight, Jack had done time with, or for, every member of that crew. They all had. It was not the blind bullshit loyalty and devotion required by a gang. They had loyalty based on lifelong bonds, and the lack of expectations upon one another made their devotion to each other implicit. When Ron's ex-girlfriend overdosed on his heroin, her brother had beaten Ron half to death. Jack had caught up with the brother about a week later and used an aluminum baseball bat to put him into the hospital and give him a permanent limp.

Ron had kept his mouth shut, and Jack had never done time for that. The cops had known it was one of them, but nobody had talked, and they couldn't charge them. Ron hadn't asked Jack to do it, and Jack had never asked Ron to keep his mouth shut when the cops came around. As a matter of fact, no words had ever been spoken about it, then or after. It had just happened. That was how it always worked, and when people forged bonds of trust with violence and love, those bonds lasted.

The crew had sort of split in the last few years. They'd gone their separate ways, but Jack and Todd were mostly still around Tacoma. Todd wasn't up to much. Neither was Jack.

Mike had been dead for several years by that time. Before he had died, he'd gotten himself a girlfriend and a job and had been taking his best shot at domesticity before really rapidly deteriorating in the months after that girlfriend had taken off. They spent a lot of time talking about Mike that afternoon, and of course Todd marched out several Mike-inspired relics from his museum of loserdom for them to reminisce over.

Ron had recently done some time at Walla Walla State Penitentiary and left the state when he was released last year. Todd told Jack that Ron was living in a small city in Northern California called Grass Valley, ironically selling weed. By that time, Ron had done some time at a few Washington State penitentiaries. They'd all done some time, but Ron more so and more recently than the others.

They called Ron that day, but nobody picked up. Jack updated Todd on what he'd been up to as much for his own information as for the next time somebody asked about Jack Todd would know what to tell them. Collecting SSI checks and living in low-income housing downtown wouldn't sound so great in most circles, but considering Jack's peers, it wasn't so bad.

It never ceased to amaze Jack how little things ever changed inside the confines of Todd's tiny house. Even Todd himself seemed frozen in time, same t-shirt and jeans, same half pack of full-flavor GPC kings sitting on the coffee table. Five years earlier that place looked just the same. It would probably look just the same five years from then. Todd broke out the bong as soon as Jack showed up. Within a few minutes, Jack was so stoned that he started to really realize how it was that time stood still in that house. For all he knew he could have been there for ten minutes or ten hours. After the first bong hit, everything had gone fast and gray. In reality, Jack had been there about two hours, and if Todd hadn't asked Jack if he wanted a ride home, he could have been there for two days.

It would have taken a couple of trips to get the records home on the bus. Jack had a lot of records. Even after trading a couple of the gems of his collection to Todd for a quarter ounce of chronic, he still had a lot of records. It didn't matter to Jack; Rodney on the Roq and DOA's Something Better Change for quarter ounce was a good deal. Jack didn't ask for a ride; Todd just offered it.

The weed was good, Jack already knew that. They smoked another bowl while they were loading Jack's records into the back of Todd's Civic hatchback. By the time they'd gotten in the car, Jack was so baked that he had a hard time figuring out how to roll the car window down. Todd didn't seem that stoned to Jack, but Todd never seemed that stoned. Todd was one of those guys that always seemed sort of stoned, never really stoned. That was convenient, since Todd was always sort of stoned. Jack was more than sort of stoned, and to him the world was humming, and he was parched.

It only took about five minutes to get back to Jack's apartment building, and Todd found a loading zone in front of the building so that he could park and help Jack bring his records up. Todd had a look at Jack's place, but he didn't stay long. He could have. He could have moved his car to a regular parking space, come back up, and smoked a while, listened to some records, but he hadn't. It was pretty clear to Jack that his unannounced arrival at Todd's had preempted something that Todd was supposed to be doing, but when one of the crew showed up on your doorstep, everything else got pushed to the back of the line. That was exactly what had happened that day. If Jack had showed up on Todd's doorstep with a bag of his clothes and no money, Todd would have let Jack stay on his couch for as long as needed, no questions asked.

There were times in the past where Todd had come over to Jack's place for a smoke and wound up moving in for six months, and other times where they hadn't seen each other for over a year. That day they hadn't said *let's hang out, or I'll call you.* They never did. They never had to. For the first time in years, they lived pretty close to one another, but proximity wasn't what kept them close. Near or far, Jack and Todd would see each other when they needed to, no words necessary.

Chapter 7

D olores worked at Grounds for Coffee. Jack tried to stop by every couple of days for a latte. Sometimes she wasn't there. That annoyed Jack. On that day, he'd already ordered a four-dollar latte before he realized she wasn't there. After he put a dollar in the tip jar, Jack was out five bucks. That annoyed Jack even more than the fact that Dolores wasn't there. Jack knew you always tipped at a place where someone you liked worked, even when they were not there, so once he'd bought the latte, he had committed to the dollar tip.

Jack had used to emphasize that point pretty regularly. "Cheap never works with girls. Also, don't haggle with call girls over their prices. It annoys 'em, and that annoyance definitely shows up in their performance. Even if the girl you like works somewhere you can't leave a tip, you still buy somethin'. If she works at a movie theater, buy a movie ticket, or at the very least get some quarters to play video games." Jack knew you needed a girl's friends and coworkers to know you weren't cheap. That approach was the main reason Jack didn't have much luck with real estate agents and girls that worked at BMW dealerships.

Jack imagined he knew Dolores. He mentally framed her as the girl at her workplace that didn't quite click with the other employees. Tragically unique. She was too cool, too aloof, or too insecure. At a hip coffee shop like that, all the employees hung out together, partied together, and knew each other's boyfriends and girlfriends. She always got invited, but she never went. Then, she went home by herself and wondered why she never hung out with her coworkers. She probably thought that they just asked her out to be nice, but didn't really want her to go. Actually, they wondered what was the matter with them when she didn't show up at all. They wanted her, and she didn't want anything to do with them. It was a John Hughes movie in the making. Regardless, Jack needed some mental framing for his masturbation session later. "Cause jerkin' it feels better when you have some context even if you have to invent that context yourself."

One day while Dolores was making Jack's latte, a thought occurred to him: He'd never seen Dolores out of her apron, and that if they ever went on a date, he'd expect her to be wearing an apron. It was possible that fifteen years of drug and alcohol abuse had damaged Jack's imagination. Jack couldn't even pretend to get to know her unless he was sitting at the coffee shop. Whenever he tried to imagine her when he was sitting in his apartment, he would just get distracted by something or fall asleep. As a way to picture her out of the apron, he started trying to think of her in something else. His problem was that all he could come up with were work uniforms. Jack had never seen her do anything except work. Again, Jack's imagination, as well as much of the remainder of his brain, had likely been significantly and permanently compromised.

What his imagination was able to produce was bizarre at best. When she handed him his latte, he saw her as a banquet waitress, then a car mechanic, next a pharmacist, then a huge step down to McDonald's shift manager, and, finally, a park ranger. In each incarnation, she was doing something appropriate to the uniform. The waitress was putting a plate of food in front of him. The car mechanic was showing him a broken alternator. The McDonald's shift manager gave him a Big Mac. The park ranger told him, "You can't camp here!" However, the pharmacist was the hottest because she was giving him Vicodin. Who wouldn't want a girlfriend whose job was to give you narcotics?

It was an inconvenient time for an acid flashback, but nonetheless it had snuck up on him, so Jack managed a thank you and quickly made his way to an empty table.

From the relative safety of his favorite table, he could observe Dolores's snug pinstripe slacks. At first, his flashback compelled him to sit down in the first open chair he spotted, but once he'd gotten his bearings, he quietly moved to his preferred table in the back of the elevated part of the dining room. That was the best vantage point for creepy stalker patrons to leer at baristas. Jack wondered if the baristas were wise to that fact.

Dolores wore that pair of pants to work about twice a week, and those were Jack's favorite days. Her hips made the pinstripes bend out and curve just a little bit. That pair was about a size smaller than her other pants, so those stripes bent a little more than they were designed to. Sometimes, when Jack was drunk, he used to like to talk about tight pants. His thoughts on the matter were fairly simple and straightforward. "No one ever said make 'em looser! That's what I'm talkin' 'bout! Right!"

That day, Jack utilized the time he didn't spend staring at Dolores's pinstripes to add to her imaginary life story. He decided she'd started, but not finished, community college, and only worked part time here, because she intended on going back to finish. She's didn't make enough money to go shopping for new clothes nearly enough, so she bought clothes that were flattering and had maximum utility, such as those pinstripe slacks. "Because those pants were built to last." And, clearly, she had great taste in music. Jack would never daydream about and pretend to date a girl who didn't have great taste in music. Of course, she was always reading an interesting book, and had just the right tattoos in just the right places. It went without saying that she would need great balance to stay atop the pedestal Jack had built to keep her on.

A few days after the acid flashback incident, Jack was back at Grounds for Coffee. That was the first day Jack had walked in and sort of wished Dolores wasn't there. Right then, he was so stoned that the best he could do was to not say anything, and the worst he could do was seem like a stoned moron. In years past, Jack could have made stoned moron cute, but he was in his late twenties, and that shit had long since worn thin. It didn't stop him from being a stoned moron. It's just that nobody thought it was cute anymore. That day, he really just wanted a five-dollar coffee, and some water, and a muffin, and a sugar cookie with the pink frosting and sprinkles on top, and a scone, and one of those slices of dried brown bread that they keep in a jar. "What the fuck are those things? I've always wanted to ask. I think they dip 'em in their coffees."

That day, she was laughing. Jack had never

imagined her laughing and he'd certainly never seen it. He took a mental picture to add to the imaginary personality he'd built for her in his head. Her laughing actually snapped him out of his stoned euphoria. She had the same short pixie cut, but, though her bangs had been fire engine red earlier that week, that day they were blue. The remainder of her hair was a mix of her natural brown roots and platinum-bleached ends, the remnants of a previous hair incarnation that she'd neglected to update. Jack wanted to compliment her new color, but she was laughing, and then he was drooling at the pastry case again, and before he knew it, the moment had passed. Apparently, pastries were a greater force than love. But, that day, despite Jack's pastry envy and blank stare, fate intervened and saved him from himself. For a moment, Jack wondered if being a stoned moron was having a renaissance.

"Do you want something out of there?"

"Yeah, I want all of it," Jack said.

"Why don't you start with some of it, and if you're still hungry, come back for the rest."

Dolores lingered in that uncomfortable way that people do when an interaction is over but there was nowhere to go. She worked there, and part of her job was waiting on him, and he, well, he was stoned out of his gourd and ravenous. Eventually, she broke the awkward silence. Whether it was ten seconds or ten minutes, Jack couldn't tell.

"You come in here all the time, you might as well tell me your name."

In his head, Jack spoke, but he must not have, because she asked him again.

"Say again. Your mouth moved, but no noise came out," she said.

When Jack did finally speak, he wished he hadn't.

"Sometimes I have to remind myself to speak out loud, but only when I'm really fuckin' stoned. I'm Jack. Did I speak that time?"

Her eyebrows raised. "That, I heard."

She smiled just slightly before walking off to help another customer. Jack assumed that was the last interaction he and Dolores would ever have.

Chapter 8

J ack's most confusing thoughts always dressed up like strange visitors, and they came over to have conversations at the most inconvenient times. "They don't speak straight! It's all garbled and stuff." Those thoughts were just riddles to him. Jack was terrified of his mind and the real people it dressed itself up as. Jack was terrified of most things, but his mind was the scariest place on earth. One thing was certain, strange visitors always meant change was on its way.

Jack was scared that night. He was as scared as he had been that time he had found an old roll of 110 Kodak film crammed in the back of a kitchen cabinet in an apartment he'd just moved into. He had driven around for two hours trying to find a one-hour photo place to develop it. That 110 film had been more or less a dead medium even back then. He eventually had found a one-hour place that still had developing equipment for the 110 film. When he had gone to pick up the prints, the person at the photo place had worn a very strange look on his face. He had handed the developed prints of that film to Jack.

What Jack had seen on those prints was morbid. Jack had only seen those types of post-mortem child photographs in documentaries on PBS. Nonetheless, there they had been, like some Victorian death photo album: a little boy, about twelve, wearing a blue suit, lying in a pine box. Based on the décor and the boy's clothes, Jack speculated this boy's funeral had taken place sometime in the mid-seventies. Jack spent enough time wrestling with the ghosts that were already in his mind. He hadn't needed an adolescent boy apparition as well. He had burned the film and prints straight away.

The year before that, Jack's father had come to visit late one night. When he had showed up, Jack had thought he was still asleep because he didn't remember letting his father in. Jack had been sitting in his chair in the living room. The two of them had just sat there watching TV at two-thirty in the morning. If the time wasn't strange enough, the fact that Jack's father had been at his place at all was. Jack's father never came any place where Jack lived, and he certainly didn't hang around and watch TV. It had been a while since he'd seen his father. Jack knew it was because his father had actually been gone for quite a while. As always, they'd parted on bad terms the last time they had seen each other.

Jack's father had appeared physically solid but a little older than the last time Jack had seen him. Jack's father wasn't overly intimidating in appearance; he was more an obvious example of the strong physical specimen that almost all blue-collar middle-aged men became. Jack's father had a head full of salt and pepper hair, calloused skin, and pear-shaped biceps. His shoulders chest and back muscles stretched and contorted the natural shape of his shirt, but his slight paunch signaled that he was just a humble working man. His standard attire was work boots, jeans, and a t-shirt. They resembled each other just slightly but only in the face.

Over the prior several years, it had become impossible for Jack to talk to his father without it turning into a lecture, a row, or, sometimes, an actual fight. For once, it had been nice to just sit and hang out with him, like they had when Jack had been a kid. They had talked like they had used to before the onset of Jack's difficulties, before Jack had become different, before he had become somebody that his father didn't accept as proper offspring of his hard-working gene pool.

They had talked about nothing in particular, but they had done so kindly, and for a long time. After an even longer time, and during one of those seven-minute lulls, Jack's father had told him that he was proud to have him as a son no matter what he did with his life. Jack's father had apologized for not standing by him before. Then he had told Jack it was late, and he needed to go and pick up Jack's mom. When he had left, it had still been two-thirty.

When he had left, Jack had known that had been the last conversation he'd have with his father. Jack was pretty sure that the conversation they'd had years back before he passed away was the last conversation they'd have, but nonetheless there he was that night.

Jack had so many varieties of fear, he rarely bothered trying to categorize, name, or even remember the underlying events attached to those fears. This fear had been different. It had not been self-centered the way most of his fears were. It had been loss for him and others. It had been fear that choked him like a rubber band wound around a finger, cutting off the blood supply. "After he left, I popped open my last 40oz, and lit a smoke. Seein' my pap again made me forget about the horrible feelings of abandonment that I'd been havin' for several months, but just for a minute or two. Like I said, that relief didn't last. It never does. My pap was gone, and we never even got to be friends. I sure hope he came to visit me that night, but it could've just been my twisted mind tellin' me what I been waitin' years to hear. Who fuckin' knows."

At a time when Jack had been legitimately trying to get his life together, it seemed like his support system had crumbled around him. Jack had reached that time in early adulthood when the friends that he had formed bad habits with had stopped being a de facto family and daily fixtures in his life. Instead, they had started becoming people who got jobs, went to prison, or moved away.

It was also at that point in life that siblings had started getting too busy to call each other on birthdays, and information about one another was primarily conveyed through conversations with parents. Worst of all, it had been the time in life when a guy like Jack had peaked and begun the long descent to the place most people had known he was heading the whole time. His bottomed-out loser schtick had worn thin. When he had been younger, Jack had been the guy that the girls in his orbit had talked about amongst themselves. He had been the guy that got punched at the bar because some tipsy girl had told her boyfriend how hot Jack was. Now, those girls had become grown women, and he had still been a boy in an alcoholic man's body. His drinking and pill-popping had soared to new heights, and, of course, he'd just received an eviction notice.

The phone ringing had woken Jack up. It had been about three-thirty in the morning. His brother Laurence's voice had come across the line. Jack had known he wouldn't want to hear what Laurence had to say, mostly because he couldn't remember the last time he'd spoken to Laurence that he *had* wanted to. It hadn't yet become clear what variety of bullshit Laurence was bringing his way, but he had been sure it was bullshit, whatever it was. It had turned out their mom had been driving home after dropping her friend off at the airport for a red-eye flight when a drunk driver had veered into her lane and hit her head-on. She had been pronounced dead at the hospital a few minutes before, but Jack was pretty sure that she'd checked out of her body after the accident about an hour ago, when his father had come to pick her up.

Laurence had told Jack to get down to St. Joseph Hospital, then immediately changed his mind and told Jack he could take care of things there, but that he was coming by Jack's in the morning to start figuring out what to do next. Laurence had been right, of course. Jack would have been useless at the hospital, so he might as well have been useless right where he was. From Jack's apartment, he could have walked to St. Joseph in ten or fifteen minutes. Instead, he had just tilted his head back, and his eyelids had rolled down like window shutters. The abyss of unconsciousness was little refuge from his existence, but as always, he had retreated there to take whatever solace it had to offer him.

They buried her one week later, and Jack had been committed less than a week after the funeral. Playtime was over, and Jack was really on his own. Nobody really grows up until that happens. Regardless of how old you are, you aren't really an adult until your parents are gone.

For some people, growing up happened the day they were born. It was a fact of their birth. Abandoned at birth, or shortly thereafter, they grew up in foster homes, or with relatives that treated them more like lodgers than family. If they survived their adolescence and early adulthood without being killed or incarcerated for the rest of their lives, they could count themselves lucky, and certainly a cut above. Beating the odds did that for a person. Getting a job, wife, and a family of their own meant purpose and love. Those people stuck out. They're black and white, and three-dimensional, in a world full of two-dimensional people splashed with obnoxious coloring. Jack saw them everywhere, and if you were looking for them, they were easy to spot. They walked with their heads held high, and they had good reason. Again, beating the odds did that for a person.

Other people grew up during the natural course of life. Family members and friends passed on, walking in tandem with the tiny successes of life. They graduated from college; a sibling died unexpectedly.

Their first child was born; they defaulted on their first home mortgage. They retired; they put their mom in a nursing home. And so on. Life went on for most in this manner. Something like Jack's brother Laurence.

There were others who were coddled throughout their entire lives, and when reality hit, it hit all at once, and it left them bewildered. It was an unexpected slip on the invisible ice that coated the front steps of life. They were upside down and stunned before they actually knew what happened. The trouble with being taken care of was that, eventually, the person in charge of your care left or died. All that while, this person had watched over you out of love. They never imagined the disservice they were doing you by bailing you out at every turn. What they did, they had done out of love, but they had left the object of that affection unable to cope with even the most insignificant happenings of normal life.

Jack had touched his mom's hand for the last time as she lay in the casket. It had been waxy and cold. He hadn't been able to help but think of a bowl of that wax fruit that tacky people used to use to decorate their homes. It hadn't been just her hand; his whole mom had been wax fruit in a bizarre-shaped bowl. He had tried to see the wax corpse as something more than a human fiction. He had tried to see it animated, as his living mom, the way he remembered her, but he hadn't been able to. And right then he had realized he couldn't even see his own memories of her alive. That wax fruit lady had been the only image of his mom he could see, and that wax fraud would permeate all his memories of his mom for the rest of his life. When he reminisced about the Christmas morning when he had gotten an Atari, it hadn't been his mom on the couch, it had been the wax fruit lady. When she had dropped him off for his first day of high school, yep, that had been the wax fruit lady too. And so it went, on and on. He had lost his mom the week before, but he had lost his memories of her to that abomination in the box that day, and forever after.

Jack was no sociopath, and he genuinely loved his mom, but he was also a self-centered and scared child in a man's body. The fact that the mortician had turned his mom into wax fruit bothered him, but not nearly as much as the adrenaline-fueled panic attack that shot through his entire body whenever he really stopped to acknowledge what her death meant for him.

Chapter 9

At eleven years old, Jack really had no idea what the world had in store for him, but the ringing in his left ear left no doubt as to what his seventeen-year-old brother Laurence had in store for him. Eleven years of age was about the last time Jack's life had seemed normal to him. Not perfect, but basically normal.

The therapist running the group session asked questions, and then he asked another question, but in response just said "um-hmm." He did it in much the same manner that a hundred therapists had done to Jack in the past, and likely the same way that a hundred more would do in future—that is, Jack thought, if he lived long enough to see a hundred more group therapists.

Besides the sporadic 911 calls, occasional attempted knifings, and regular baseball bat duels, things had actually been pretty good between Laurence and Jack back then. Actually, occurrences of life-threatening confrontations between Laurence and Jack had been down since the summer before Jack started sixth grade.

Their mom had grown tired of sitting in the emergency room and having strangers stare at her like she was some sort of child beater, so for Christmas, Santa Claus had brought Laurence and Jack boxing gloves—pretty big ones, too. At least, they had seemed big on Jack's little hands. In retrospect, Jack couldn't tell you if they had been twelve or sixteen-ounce gloves, but Jack's gloves had been like enormous marshmallows on his hands, while Laurence's gloves had seemed like they were just thin strips of leather protecting his fists from injury.

Jack's gloves had actually been quite a bit smaller than Laurence's gloves, and that had been evident when they were sitting side by side. Jack's gloves had been a child size. Laurence's had been an adult size. Even so, Jack's little hands just hadn't filled those big, squishy marshmallows, and it had showed in his lack of punching power. Meanwhile, Laurence's gloves had struck Jack like socks full of pennies being swung at him.

Those Christmas gloves had been supposed to serve one purpose, and that had been to keep Laurence and Jack from doing any damage to each other that would result in scars or hospital visits. In that endeavor, they had achieved only tepid results. Unfortunately for Jack, that had meant semi-regular, undiagnosed mild concussions as direct results of taking too many blows from Laurence's much stronger, larger, and faster hands. The cuts and blood resulting from their brawls had been less frequent, but the intensity and length of time their battles took on had become legendary in scale. One thing had become clear to Jack very quickly: getting hit a couple hundred times in ten minutes several times a week certainly took a toll on a kid, but he could do it again and again.

Except for a white stripe over the front of them, their gloves had been a sort of a dried blood color. Jack had supposed the white strip over the front was the part of the glove that was supposed to connect at the conclusion of a well-thrown punch. The only parts of Laurence's gloves Jack had ever seen were the white stripes. Laurence had never seen the white stripes on Jack's gloves. Sometimes it had been hard for Jack to tell if he was seeing the white because Laurence's right glove was still in Jack's face or because Laurence had rung his bell so hard that he was staring at the white ceiling of their garage. Jack had devised a clever way to figure out which white he was seeing. If he had to get up off the ground it had been the latter. If not, it had been the former.

One day when Jack was sitting in his fifth-grade classroom, he had gotten out his sixty-four pack of

Crayola crayons to color something. Fifth grade had been the last year of school in which coloring was still considered schoolwork. Upon seeing a not-quite-brown and not-quite-red crayon, Jack had immediately pulled it out and said to himself: "That's the color of dried blood. The color of dried blood is the exact color of our boxing gloves." The crayon had indicated on its half-torn-off paper sleeve that it was Burnt Sienna.

Along with Jack's inability to connect a punch with Laurence's face, one of the reasons that Laurence had never seen the white stripes on Jack's gloves was that the blood gushing out of Jack's nose and mouth had covered the white stripes and dried there. Jack's gloves had been all Burnt Sienna, no white stripes remaining. Laurence's gloves had stayed clean because he hadn't pressed them into his face constantly in a futile effort to stop his nose and mouth from bleeding. Laurence's gloves had always been near his head, protecting his face. Either that, or they had been punching Jack in his.

Boxing with Laurence was about as close as Jack had ever gotten to a positive life lesson. Jack had actually learned the value of losing during those fights. He had learned the value of perseverance. If Jack could have ever applied what he had learned with those boxing gloves on, he might have been alright. He hadn't.

One day, Jack had snuck a left hook past Laurence's gloves and bloodied his nose. Jack had been too timid to even try hitting Laurence for the longest time. Hitting Laurence had seemed an insurmountable task, and so it had always seemed smarter for Jack to cover his face and mitigate the inevitable damage. That day, Jack had realized that even when he spent all his energy covering his face, he still ended up bruised and bloodied, so he had decided to try to hit Laurence. It had turned out it wasn't really that hard to hit Laurence after all. In fact, Jack had unleashed a flurry of punches culminating in that left hook, slipping by Laurence's block and breaking his nose.

That had been the last fight and the last trip to the emergency room. It had been the summer before Jack started sixth grade, and Laurence had been the one in charge of watching Jack while their mom was at work. Laurence had called their mom's work number. Jack had thought Laurence was crying, but he had run out of the room too fast to see for sure. When she had gotten home, she had almost laughed when she saw Laurence's nose. It was bent so far to the left of his face that it looked like a steamroller had come along and meticulously flattened it. Her and Jack were the only ones that could possibly have found the situation funny. Practically every day that summer, she had come home to find Jack with toilet paper shoved up his nose, or raccoon eyes. The irony that one square blow had managed to do to Laurence's nose what Laurence's fists had failed to do to Jack's nose over those last months caused a little bit of twisted joy in their mom.

The doctor had reset it, but you could still see that Laurence's nose bent off to the left side of his face a little if you were looking for it. To Jack, it was the best trophy on earth, and it would never go away, not as long as Laurence was still around.

The other patients usually just sat there and let Jack talk, even when he was rambling. They were just happy somebody was saying something. It took the focus off of them. In any normal group of people, Jack would be delighted to sit in the background and remain unnoticed, but in there he always felt a little superior, and of course that meant he suddenly had plenty to say.

Jack's anxiety and social phobia typically kept him from speaking in even small groups of normal people, but in there, in that place with all the other throwaways, he was a star. And, just like with his inability to apply those lessons he'd learned during those fights with Laurence all those years ago, he similarly failed to make use of any lessons that place might have had to teach him. Instead, he squandered his time there showboating, showing a crowd of unimpressed staff and patients how he was the best of the malfunctioning cogs.

Jack was good at sinking a few balls—hard shots, too; banks off multiple rails, stuff like that. Ironically, he always missed clear shots at the eight ball, all night long, every time. It was the most frustrating thing for people in Jack's life to watch. Watching a light go on in someone's head for a moment before they proceeded to slightly miss the mark over and over when it was time to apply what had been learned during that momentary epiphany.

Watching someone that might have made it fail was more heartbreaking than writing off the people who had never had a chance anyway. Jack was a fifty-one-card deck. He was hard to throw out, because he was so close to functional. You always thought that other card would just turn up in a junk drawer or a couch cushion, so you keep that incomplete deck in a cabinet. You kept it forever, and, of course, that missing five of spades never showed up, and looking at that fifty-one-card deck eventually became a point of frustration and resentment.

They ended group before Jack was done talking, but Jack still had a captive audience of one. Beth had been sitting in the corner listening to their group session.

Beth was more than a secondary character occupying a few forgettable pages of Jack's story. Beth was beautiful, and she was genuine, and she probably spent more time looking for that fifty-second card than anyone else in Jack's life.

Beth had heard this story before, but she intently listened as if it were the first time. She'd probably heard all Jack's stories before, but she liked hearing them again. It wasn't even the stories themselves; it was how Jack told them. He was a good storyteller, and he could tell you about sitting at the Department of Licensing for three hours and make it entertaining.

"So, what happened next?" Beth asked.

"Nothin' really, I busted Laurence's nose. I mean, he went to the doctor, and they set it and all that, but that was the last boxin' match. We still argued about petty brother shit, but no more physical altercations. Those gloves went into the closet for good after that. Eventually, they went into the garbage can when I was cleanin' some of my old shit out of my parents' place. For a minute, though, I think even my pap saw a little of himself in me. I'm sure it was just a little bit, and just for a minute, and never again. Nonetheless, it was worth a childhood full of put-downs and a summer filled with beatins'. At least I had a moment, and after that I just became who I became."

"Who did you become?" Beth's expression changed. Her eyebrows twitched upward, but just a little. It was subtle, but Jack had spent so much time by that point studying her face that he noticed any subtle change. That tiny expression meant she hadn't been expecting Jack's last statement.

Beth wasn't just humoring Jack; she really wanted to know what had brought Jack to the place he was in. She felt guilty for devoting so much attention to this one patient as she clearly and simultaneously neglected others. She felt guilty for feeling something more for this one patient than a professional caregiver should have felt. She felt guilty because she felt like she was being emotionally unfaithful to her long-time boyfriend, Tim, who really was a good guy. She felt guilty, but she kept doting, kept listening to the stories, and kept wondering what a repaired Jack could do if given the opportunity.

"You know. Whatever the fuck I am now," Jack said.

Beth was about five years older than Jack, and she'd had some interaction with him during each of his four prior visits to Western State. There may have been one or two other familiar faces amongst the staff from his first visit, but the only one he knew for a fact was there from his first time was Beth.

"I'm fuckin' scared. They're all gone. And not that bullshit momentary scared like when you have to talk in front of the class. It's scared like in my gut, and, like, all the time. It's the scared that's a constant dull ache in my stomach, not just a jolt at a horror movie. Sometimes it goes away when I'm drinkin' or fuckin', or pilled up, but rest of the time it's there. The ache is in my gut, and the thoughts are in my brain. They stick to my brain. They coat it like the way super glue coats your fingertip. The thoughts, they don't go away, they don't get tired out, they don't quit. They just win, and they make my gut ache worse.

"My family's gone, except my brother, who barely spoke to me even when our parents were alive. My only friends are either ekin' out a miserable false façade of normality or circlin' the drain right along with me. If I don't get it together this time, I think I'm done for. Dyin' don't really scare me, and it don't really bother me neither. I kind of wish it would just come already so I can get done with all this, this place, this life, this planet. Fuckers die, they don't even appreciate it. Give it to me, I'd fuckin' appreciate it. The only miserable people I know are alive. The dead ones are at rest and no doubt happy. I don't fuckin' know. I'm scared of bein' scared, and I'm scared of bein' alive. I can't kill myself, but dyin' some other way would be more easy."

"What would make you want to live, she asked."

"I don't have to be a millionaire, or famous, or even financially secure. I don't need a wife, a good job, or a house in the suburbs. I'd just like to have peace in my mind for five minutes. I'd like to live without the terror of existence that taps my brain like fuckin' non-stop war drums. Thump, thump, thump, I can't escape. It's on the move, and it's comin' after me. I'd like to feel safe and secure without the assistance of alcohol or drugs. I want to be Laurence, not Jack. Being Jack is the worst."

Beth and Jack had started at that place, but Jack hadn't known all that yet. All he had known was that the year he had turned eighteen, when he was committed to that place the first time, he'd met the only person he'd ever have a real connection with. She had known it before Jack did. She had even transferred wards and gotten off graveyard shifts to spend more time with him.

Some might call it love at first sight. It was an open question whether Jack could even understand what love between two mature people was. It was just as likely that Jack was lovable in the way that an abused dog was lovable. It was also possible that he would have become devoted to the first person to come along and toss him a bone. Whatever it was, it was certainly a meaningful connection on a level that people didn't typically understand. Some things just stick when they are thrown together, and nothing else matters. Once in your life, you might stick to someone and not be able to disentangle yourself, not that you would ever want to. If that happens, consider yourself one of the lucky ones. Beth and

Jack had stuck together. That was just how it was.

Chapter 10

Liberating his mind from Mormon indoctrination might have been the only bold stand Jack had ever taken. Abusing one's body with substances as Jack had done certainly took balls, and suffering mentally as he had done took endurance, but a stand was different. For an eleven-year-old, taking God out of your life was a big step. It was more than that; it was a stand. Liberating your mind from anything encumbering it was a step in the right direction, and a step toward owning the only thing that anyone could truly own, their own mind, couldn't ever be the wrong choice. "That is, you own it right up until the fuckin' moment you don't." Nevertheless, the mind was the last refuge. Whether the refuge held up or not is another story, but for most people, it was a domain they could own absolutely.

For Jack, that first step away from Mormonism had happened at school. Of course, it hadn't happened in a classroom, or the gym, or even the cafeteria. Like most of Jack's revelations back then, it had happened on the playground. On that occasion, school had not even been in session. It had been summer, late summer. Even summer school had been let out a few weeks before. It had probably been August, but nobody could ever know for sure.

When the playground went quiet in the late summer, the truly odd kids came out to play on it. The kids whose parents had let them walk to school in kindergarten. The kids that broke into the abandoned houses in the neighborhood for no better reason than to see what was inside. Those kids were the ones that went to the playground on days like that. Those kids didn't go there to find kids to play with. They went just to haunt an abandoned playground. Jack had been such a kid. *"The Omega Man* and *Dawn of the Dead* changed my whole perspective on shit. A world without all those pesky humans would have been a playground for me. It was my best fantasy. A playground without a bunch of kids was my best reality."

He hadn't been looking for them, but Jack had found people that day at the playground. They hadn't seemed to mind being found, either. As a matter of fact, they had seemed pretty excited at Jack's arrival. Fernando and Angelina had been in the same grade as Jack, and they'd all been in the same class more than once. Fernando had been the only Latino kid at Jack's elementary school. He had been Puerto Rican. He'd moved to the United States a few years earlier. When a new kid from somewhere interesting showed up at school, girls were always immediately interested. The Puerto Rican thing had worn off a long time before, but he had still had an accent that Jack suspected he had embellished to remind everybody that he was from someplace exotic. To eleven-year-old Jack, Puerto Rico had seemed exotic.

Angelina had been what you would call unremarkable in every way imaginable. She hadn't been popular, but she had known a few girls that she had hung around with at school. She'd had a goofy-ass little girl bowl cut which kids had made fun of and had certainly hurt her overall appearance, but she hadn't been ugly. She hadn't worn nice clothes, but the ones she had worn were clean and well-kept. Jack hadn't ever talked to her, so he had assumed she was shy, but for all he knew she could have been a horrendous bitch.

Jack had stared at that bowl cut. He'd never been that close to it. He hadn't been able to not stare at it. She may have been unremarkable, but she had also been the first girl Jack had ever smoked a joint with, and the first girl he had ever made out with. The fact that both things and more had happened on the same day had made Jack a god amongst other eleven-year-olds. That had also made Fernando the first guy Jack had ever smoked a joint with, but nobody really gave a shit about the first guy you had smoked a joint with.

That day had started the same as every other day that Jack had spent at the playground to be by himself that summer. He had liked to go to the ballfields first. They had been the first part of the school grounds that Jack had come across while walking to the school, so they had been an easy place to start. Sometimes, adults had come and played there. Adults and older kids playing on the fields would forget or lose things. Sometimes, they had just left useful things behind. Usually, it had just been sports equipment. There had been those rare occasions when somebody had taken off their watch or a ring, or better yet set a wallet on the bench by home plate.

After combing the ball fields for valuable possessions and useful castoffs Jack would head over to the swings to comb through the grass behind them and see what had shaken out the pants pockets of those who had been swinging. The last stop on his tour of the playground had always been a unique feature that not all playgrounds had. There had been a gigantic gravel pit next to the portables where the kindergarten kids had gone to class. That had been where the big toys were. The gravel pit had always been good for a few things. There had almost always been a couple of *Star Wars* action figures or some Hot Wheels cars that kids had lost. There had never been anything great, but there had always been something worth taking home.

The tire mountain had never had anything worth taking home, but it was always worth looking inside of it. The thing had been unavoidable. It called out to you. A mountain constructed entirely of gigantic tractor tires large enough for grown men to climb inside of and sit down. Judging from the items regularly left behind in the tires, it appeared they had also been large enough inside for grown men to drink Jack Daniels, smoke cigarettes, shoot IV drugs, and pass out in pools of puke. Venturing into the tires was always a trip into the unknown. Normally, Jack would find a dormant, transient body curled around a nearly empty bottle of Night Train or the aforementioned Jack Daniels. That day, all he had found was Fernando and Angelina.

Jack had seen the joint they were holding. They hadn't mustered up the nerve to light it. Jack had been all in the second he saw the thing. They hadn't been expecting Jack to show up. For whatever reason, they had seemed to think that Jack had smoked a joint before and would be able to show them how. Jack had ended up being the one to light it up and take the first hit. It had tasted like he was smoking perfume made from pond scum.

He had inhaled the smoke and held it in like he'd seen Cheech do on *Up in Smoke.* Jack had known immediately that he was in love. As he had exhaled, he had felt electric sensations running up the various blood vessels in his head. It had felt like when you stood up too fast, but much more intense.

Fernando had taken a couple of puffs, but Jack didn't think he had really even inhaled it. Angelina and Jack had smoked the rest of the joint, which Fernando had lifted from his older brother's room. After it was gone, they had been really baked. Jack had an even harder time not staring at Angelina's bowl cut. To Jack's stoned mind, it had seemed more like some sort of animal that had taken residence on top of her head than a haircut.

It turned out that Fernando had actually taken the joint from his brother's room because Angelina was his across the street neighbor, and he'd told her that his brother always had joints in his room. She had told him to get one so that they could smoke it. Of course, he had wanted to impress the neighbor girl, and next thing they knew they were sitting in the tire mountain. That was when Jack had showed up.

After they had smoked the joint, Fernando had seemed to go crazy. Contact high, Jack had guessed. Jack doubted he'd had a real hit of the thing at all. Jack had felt crazy too, but he had maintained his composure because there had been a girl there. Just like at home when Lisa, his hot babysitter, would come over. He had always had to take a dump because his mom had made macaroni and cheese with hot dogs in it for dinner whenever she had left him with a babysitter. It had been just like that. He'd had to eat, so he had eaten, then he'd had to shit, so he had shit.

"You got to get to that bathroom and do your thing, but you got to maintain your cool. You can't be poopin' yourself while you're sitting on the couch watchin' the movie with the hot babysitter. You can't even fart into the cushion, too risky. There's always smell leakage. I'd risk it if it was just my mom or Laurence, but not when Lisa was there. Eventually, though, you got to make your move for the bathroom. The best time was like halfway through the movie, right after Lisa went in and peed out the Tab she'd been drinking. Plus, as an added bonus, the bathroom had a faint hint of what girls smell like after they pull down their jeans. It was sweet and sour."

Fernando hadn't maintained his composure. He had just gone bonkers and run away. Fernando had been the kind of kid that pooped at the wrong time when the hot babysitter was over. It had taken about thirty seconds before Jack completely stopped worrying about what had happened to Fernando. It had probably been another full minute before Jack had forgotten that Fernando existed at all, and about five minutes after that he forgot the entire rest of the world had existed at all. Nothing outside of the tire mountain had mattered, and Jack had become convinced that nothing out there was real anyway.

It was very deep introspection, but very insignificant when you realized that every other eleven-year-old kid who had smoked a joint, or taken a hit of acid, had had the exact same experience. While that may have been true, those other eleven-year-olds hadn't had a hot bowl cut girl like Angelina inside a gigantic tractor tire. Or maybe they did, but Angelina had been Jack's hot bowl cut girl.

Being eleven, stoned out of your mind, and stuck in a universe that consisted of the inside of a gigantic tractor tire had a way of breaking down barriers that kept eleven-year-old kids from touching each others' private parts. Angelina had started talking about what it would be like if they touched certain parts of each other's bodies. Jack had begun to feel even stranger than he already had from the weed, so he had just reached out and grabbed one of Angelina's boobs. Or at least, he had grabbed what would someday be a boob. Still, he had known he was getting somewhere, and he had gotten two full fingers full of nipple.

Jack had been content to keep touching nipple over her shirt because she had kept acting like she was enjoying it. Then she had done something unexpected. She had stuck her hand in Jack's jeans and grabbed his hard cock and slid her tongue in his mouth. Jack had kissed her back and immediately stuck his hand inside the waistband of her shorts. He had felt wetness, and he had smelt that sweet and sour smell that his babysitter left in the bathroom, but much stronger. Without even trying, Jack had gotten to third base. He hadn't even known what that meant, but she had seemed content. Jack had cummed a few seconds later, which had immediately answered for him a long-standing question: what exactly was an erection good for? When Jack had been little, he had used to wonder why God had created a body part as useless as a dick. Weren't there a hundred other more efficient ways to move urine out of the body? Jack hadn't known every-thing, but he had known that girls didn't have dicks, and they seemed to manage peeing just fine. Jack had known this because he'd been in the women's restroom at the Bon Marché numerous times with his mom when he had been much younger. When he had been little, and he needed help going, she had brought him into the women's restroom. All the women in the bathroom seemed like they peed out of their butts just fine. Needless to say, it had been epiphany central in the gigantic tractor tire that afternoon.

After Jack came, the mood in the tire had changed. Jack had still been really high, but Angelina had looked at him like she had done something wrong. Jack hadn't really understood why the mood had changed; he just knew it had. As far as he was concerned it had been a perfect day. He had gotten baked for the first time, and he'd had his first hand job. It had lasted all of ten seconds, but Jack figured endurance would come with more practice. Jack had started to think about heading home. He had figured the afternoon cartoons would be coming on soon and he hadn't wanted to miss Star Blazers. He had told Angelina that he was going to head back to his house, and that she could come watch cartoons if she wanted. She had just shaken her head.All of a sudden, conversation had stopped, physical interaction had stopped, fun had stopped, and weirdness had begun. Jack had asked if she was okay to walk home, and she had nodded.

This is a scenario that would play out again and again with every girl Jack ever had sex with. Except for Beth. There were intimacy problems from the start, but never with Beth. For some reason, Jack immediately got the feeling that he owed Angelina something, but he wasn't sure what was expected of him. He had wanted to leave because he hadn't known what would make things feel normal again. He had wanted to put distance between him and the weirdness. So was born Jack's postcoital routine. For most of Jack's life, he had been more comfortable paying for sex because he knew exactly what the girl wanted: the money. It was a transaction, and everybody walked away with what they bargained for. Jack really believed that. That was one of the reasons he had never tried to lowball working girls. He figured if they were nice enough to bang the guys they were expected to bang to make ends meet, they'd earned every penny of it.

At night, Jack would sneak out of the house and roam the local alleys in his neighborhood. In his house, he could have walked right out the front door, and no one would have even noticed. His dad couldn't have cared less what Jack did, his mom was always asleep on the couch in the evening, and it was doubtful his brother would have even noticed. It was even more doubtful that any of them would have given a crap if they had noticed. Nonetheless, Jack had employed covert tactics.

His room on the second floor had had a laundry chute in it. Basically, it had been a smelly hole where people had dropped dirty clothes into a compart- ment that looked like a cabinet in the laundry room on the first floor. There had been a flip top lid on the chute that had stanched some of the smell, but a week of a family's dirty clothes sitting just below your bedroom had a sour stench all the same.

Where others only recognized the ripe stink of dirty underwear, Jack had recognized opportunity. The chute had gone straight down, and it was only about six or seven feet from top to bottom, so one day Jack had tried lowering himself down it. After that, Jack would turn on his TV, turn out his light, and lock his door before exiting the house through the chute. Since he had always slept with his TV on and his door locked, no one would think anything strange was up if they came by his door.

Jack would brace the rubber soles of his Sauconys on the side walls of the chute, grip the rim of the chute, and lower himself down slowly. From there, popping the chute door open from the inside and lowering himself onto the washing machine had been no problem. The back door to the house had been in the laundry room, and no one ever locked any of the doors at Jack's house, so reentry was guaranteed. Even if it hadn't been, there had been at least five windows on the ground floor that didn't lock at all. Getting back up the chute was a little more time-consuming, as he'd had to brace his shoes against the walls of the chute so he could inch his way back up, but it really hadn't been any more complicated than getting down, just more intensive. This was how young Jack had gained absolute freedom of movement.

Dragging his Radio Flyer red wagon behind him,

he would snatch the aluminum cans other families had been collecting for recycling. They'd leave them by their garages, on their back porches; anywhere Jack wouldn't have to breach a lock to get at their cans made them fair game. Jack's covert tactics had cost him a few bite wounds from filthy canine mongrels, but he had always been victorious in the end. Sometimes he had recycled newspapers as well, but they were bulky and hadn't paid out the way cans did. Also, when they got wet, none of the recycling places had wanted them. The recycling places not taking wet newspapers had sort of been a coffin nail to Jack getting seriously involved in the newspaper game, as he had pulled his goods in a little red wagon in Washington where it rained even when the sun was out. Still, if he found a motherload of newspapers under a carport, he would still grab them and gamble that he'd get them to the recycling center mostly dry.

Because of cans, Jack had always had a pocketful of cash, usually six or seven dollars. On that day, he had needed it because he had felt compelled to bring Angelina to the Korean lady's candy store by the school for candy and soda. Jack had gone to that store almost daily for years. He must have dropped a thousand dollars into the Frogger machine at that little store, but he had never known the woman who owned it by anything other than Korean lady, which could be confusing since he had lived in a neighborhood that was about a third Korean.

As a matter of fact, his friend that lived five blocks north of him had gone to a similar store by his house that was owned by a Korean lady, and he had called that store the Korean lady's candy store, too. In Alabama, if you said "the Korean lady," everybody knew who you were talking about, since there were probably all of three Korean ladies in the whole state. In south Tacoma, the Korean lady could have been anyone.

Jack was white, but when he was little, his two best friends had been Korean. Most of the small businesses in his neighborhood were owned and operated by Korean people. There had been Korean writing all over signs and business banners in his neighborhood, all of which seemed perfectly normal to him until that day. Jack had started to wonder if the Korean lady at the store referred to him as the white kid that always played Frogger. He had started to wonder why he called her the Korean lady, instead of just the lady at the candy store. He had figured there was something more there to think on, but his brain had been mushy right then, and he hadn't been able to formulate coherent thoughts anymore.

Still high, but now convinced that the world outside might actually exist, and be safe, they had ventured out. For a while, Jack had really considered never leaving the apparent calm and safety of the tire. Even at that age, Jack figured that if a girl gave him sexual attention, he should buy her something. Walking through the door, Jack had asked Angelina if he should get some quarters for Frogger or Pac-Man. She had declined, but he had offered, and to Jack, as long as he got credit for asking, that was all that mattered. Once they were in the store, Jack had told Angelina that she could get whatever she wanted, and however much she wanted of it. Jack had grabbed two Charleston Chews, a Three Musketeers, and a Coke. She had opted for an ice cream sandwich, and an A&W Root Beer.

Outside the store, Jack had enjoyed the best meal he'd ever had, then or since. Angelina had nibbled at her ice cream sandwich and barely sipped the root beer. Five minutes later, Jack had felt the way he'd felt for the eleven years previous to the joint: bland, normal, shy, bored, depressed, and embarrassed. Even so, he had offered to walk Angelina home, but she had preferred to walk alone. She had lived in the opposite direction, so Jack had been happy to let her go. Plus, he had figured her parents would know what they'd done if he showed up with her. Jack had imagined the events in the tire would play like a movie projecting on his forehead for everyone to see. He had envisioned Angelina's dad as a big burly man, and upon his arrival at her house, he'd scream "did you just fuck around with my daughter" right in Jack's face. That was actually the nice version of what he had envisioned her father would do after seeing the pornographic tire mountain movie on his forehead.

Jack had just said, "see you later," and watched her walk off down Park Avenue. He'd see her from time to time for the next several years, but they had never really talked again. "Hi" or an awkward "how's it going" was about all they were ever able to muster after that. Eventually she grew the bowl cut out, and Jack realized she was more attractive than he'd initially thought. Luckily, they'd had nothing before that joint, so it hadn't been much of a loss that they had nothing after it, either. Right then, it had occurred to Jack that, if he ran home, he could probably catch the last half of Star Blazers.

Chapter 11

I n retrospect, Jack could admit that being committed at eighteen had advantages that being committed at twenty-eight did not. To start, when he was eighteen, he had still been able to remember what being with Angelina in the tire had felt like.

By twenty-eight, the visceral feeling of that experience had disintegrated into a worn-out Betamax tape version of itself. Sure, you could still watch the *Stand by Me* tape you'd watched a thousand times, but all the sharpness was gone. Not only that, but there were entire portions of the tape that were just snow on the screen, eaten, crumpled tape. The experience was nothing that was really real to Jack at the age of twenty-eight. It might as well have been someone else's memory, or for that matter an actual movie on a worn-out Betamax tape.

Jack sat and wondered how many of his real memories were really real at all, or if he'd just told himself a particular lie so many times that his brain had accepted it as the truth. He figured that most of his memories had started out as real events and received some embellishments shortly thereafter to increase the curb appeal to other people who might hear the memory as a story Jack told at some point. However, the pristine, if somewhat embellished, final theatrical release version of the memories were ultimately altered and degraded through the telling and retelling of them. "It's the Betamax tape that got played over and over. By the way I'm the one who came up with that Betamax metaphor thing, not him. I just told him about it one time, and now he uses it all the time like he thought it up."

Jack also figured there was a bit of collective memory that was appropriated to oneself. "Because that reminds me of the time that I was super wasted, and I boned that girl Cherise, but then I ran into that dude Phil like a year later, and it turned out that he boned her. I was just there in the bed half asleep. Man, I was sure I boned her, but it turns out it was Phil." Jack was so upset about it that he had called Cherise after he had found out. They had hooked up shortly after that. Apparently, he felt he'd lost something when he found out he hadn't had sex with her, and just really wanted to get it back. A notch on his bedpost had been subtracted, and he couldn't mentally square it being gone, so he'd had to make it the truth.

None of that had helped him ask Dolores out on

a date that day. Stories of pre-teen ejaculation, post-teen institutional commitment, sibling brutality, and an inability to discern his own memories from those of his friends weren't good icebreakers with female baristas. At least, he assumed they weren't. Jack lacked real dating experience. For instance, when he had called up Cherise, he had just asked her if she wanted to watch a movie. He had showed up at her apartment with a case of Schmidt Ice, and a VHS of *Clerks*.

Two hours later, it had been on. Two hours and ten minutes later, he had felt guilty. He had wanted to leave, so he had left the open pack of Camels on her bedside table and the rest of the beer in the fridge. He had taken the *Clerks* tape, since he used it pretty regularly to hook up with girls, but he had figured the beer and smokes were an appropriate illustration of his gratitude for a good time. He had seen her a couple years later at a show. She had been with some guy. She had said "hey" when Jack walked by, but other than that ignored him. At that point, he had figured that the beer and smokes must not have been enough gratitude for Cherise, and wondered if maybe he should have left the *Clerks* VHS at her place, too.

There were plenty of baristas that were into beer and sloppy hook ups, but Dolores didn't seem like one of them. Jack was scared of pretty much everything already. Talking to girls wasn't typically on the list, but it was that day. Since Dolores couldn't be wooed by a case of cheap beer and a movie, he was very far out of his element. He'd spent two months going to Grounds for Coffee almost every day to see Dolores. It certainly wasn't for the overpriced, pretentious coffee. Jack usually went home afterward, where his only window pointed at the coffee shop. Jack could see Dolores inside working for the rest of her shift.

Jack pumped himself up to ask her out. "She was probably insulted that I hadn't asked her out. She probably thought somethin' was wrong with her because even the guy that lived in the low-income apartments that spent all his SSI money on coffee wouldn't even ask her out." As soon as Jack felt the requisite amount of courage to go through with it, his brain would drag him right back down. Jack didn't bring much to the table as a potential mate. Unfortunately for Jack, that was exactly what he said to her the following day.

She was doing a "find your ideal mate" quiz in *Cosmopolitan* when he walked in to order his morning coffee at one in the afternoon.

"What do you bring to a relationship as a potential mate, Jack?" At first, he thought she was being glib, but she looked genuinely interested in getting his response.

"Well, I'd bring my SSI check every month, and make sure the house is clean. I've been with a lot of girls, but I don't have a lot of relationship experience per se—" (he added air quotes when he said "relationship") "—but I have a sincere desire to have a lastin' connection with another human being."

Her mouth hung open like she was about to say "wow" in a get me the fuck out of here sort of way. Jack figured that at any second she was going to start backing away from the counter to put some space between them before realizing she was sort of trapped in a fairly confined coffee shop with him. In reality, she thought he might be the funniest person she'd ever met. She couldn't figure out how he'd come up with such a great response so fast. She was quite impressed with his ability to fabricate such a clever retort to the ridiculousness of a cosmo quiz with an equally ridiculous and contrary response. Dolores had been attracted to him before, but with that one brazen show of wit, he was fifty percent more attractive immediately.

It was unfortunate for Dolores that she couldn't recognize a person who had just dumped too much crazy and too much honesty on her the way a five-year-old sheepishly admits to eating all the cookies.

"Wow, that's a mouthful. All this stupid quiz says is to look for somebody who puts down the toilet seat and has a job," she said.

Jack hadn't seen the magazine until after he was done speaking. He thought she was asking him to apply for the position of her boyfriend, just like that, right there in that coffee shop.

Jack replied as confidently as anyone could in such an embarrassing circumstance. "Well, I have one of those things goin' for me, but it's not the job." Then he frowned.

Jack had employed many strange techniques with the opposite sex, and he'd had many of them work, but he'd never used the crippled angel routine. It wasn't a routine, though. Jack needed somebody right at that moment. He'd just spent Thanksgiving, not two weeks earlier, eating turkey sandwiches made from cold cuts he had bought at the store with his food stamps. They weren't even the good cold cuts from the deli counter. They were the shitty packaged ones in the refrigerated aisle of the store. He needed somebody to give him a chance to start getting somewhere. He'd done the best he could do for himself, without help, and failed pretty miserably. On his own, all he'd been able to manage was a crappy apartment, a monthly check from the state, and endless hours with which to contemplate what to do with the next allotment of endless hours.

He didn't need something; he needed somebody, just like he always had. People had always been the only stability in his life, and all his people were gone. Jack figured that if he could just make a start with someone that was willing to believe that he could be more than he was at that moment, he might be okay. He needed somebody that saw a project, not a lost cause. Jack wondered if Dolores could be that girl. Jack assumed it wouldn't ultimately matter, as he could never overcome his ill-advised disclosures to her. "It's like takin' a dump at a girl's place the first time she invites you over. You just can't come back from one of those!"

"I know you like coffee because I see you in here almost every day. What else do you like? What do you do when you're not in here drinking coffee" she asked.

Jack almost said, "I sleep eighteen hours a day because I'm broke as a joke and spend all my spare money on this outrageously expensive coffee so that I can talk to you for sixty seconds," but his common sense had finally caught up to his mouth, and he stayed quiet for a minute.

Finally, Jack spoke. "Honestly, I don't do much, but I like you. I like you a lot, and I'm just tryin' to figure out how selfish it is for me to impose myself and my issues on someone else."

"Well, my life is already coasting in neutral, so now's a good time for you to hop on. Do you feel like hopping on, Jack?"

There was some definite innuendo to that last little part. Jack could tell by the way she leaned forward and let him get a good look at her cleavage when she said it.

"All I can do is slow you down, and all you can do is break my heart," Jack said.

"Well, then, why don't we try having a little fun before we start destroying each other's lives?"

Jack figured he had no business going out on a date with a girl, even if said girl was unwise enough to agree to go. Dating was the sort of thing people with jobs, cars, and decent apartments did. All he wanted right then was to take this girl out, but he had a hard time justifying it in his mind. Jack decided to waste his entire month's spending money, which he had rationed so carefully from his government issued SSI check, on one night out with Dolores. He wasn't even trying to get laid. If he was, using all his spending money might actually make sense. He just wanted to take her out on a nice little date; dinner, movie, whatever.

Here he was again, imposing his poor circum-stances upon another. This other didn't even really know what she was in for. She still thought his approach was some schtick or something, and he was about to blow all his spending money for the month keeping up that façade. She had passed on his clear offers to withdraw and leave her in peace, but he knew she couldn't possibly know how bad of shape he was really in. So it didn't seem right from the outset, but Jack wanted it so badly that he forced the quieting of his forebodings.

He knew it was selfish, but he pushed that down anyhow. He needed this. He needed a lifeline. He needed something to leech off of for a while so that he could feel partially human again. Whenever Jack sucked, he had a bad habit of leaving a dried-out husk behind. Most of his husks knew what they were getting into right up front, so he'd always been able to tell himself he wasn't really a bad guy, but Dolores was different. She was about to be sucked dry without proper notification. Jack knew that, and he felt bad about it, but Jack had to look out for Jack first and foremost, so he did it anyway.

In fairness, if you had to judge Jack, you wouldn't call him a bad guy. He was certainly selfish. He was fearful of life, so fearful, in fact, that, to him, his existence seemed more like walking through a real-life horror movie than a real life at all. That also made him extremely paranoid. Outwardly, any casual observer could characterize him as a train wreck simply on the basis of his substance abuse alone. He used people, and in the process often used them up, but his goal was not to destroy them, not even close. Jack was just a germ with feelings, and germs destroyed things. He wasn't a sociopath, and he didn't like it, but germs destroyed things. That's just what they did. That's what he did.

Jack was actually giddy planning out his date with Dolores. He really had no idea what a "good date" consisted of. Jack always did finger quotes when he said "good date." He knew dinner and a movie, but what restaurant? What was the dress code for a "good date?" How much full-frontal nudity was appropriate for a "good date" movie? The Mecca Theater in downtown Tacoma, which was right next door to his apartment building and across the street from Grounds for Coffee, had movies, but they were of the XXX variety. He supposed the Mecca was not a good choice for a movie on a first date, but the location was convenient. Plus, they sold cigarettes at the counter and you could smoke in the theater. Those were the upsides. The downsides were, again, that all they played were pornographic feature films, the employees were perverts, and the theater smelled like cum. "Not only that, but there was always a fifteen-year-old male prostitute suckin' off some scuzzy seventy-year-old man two rows in front of you."

For all Jack knew about dating, you took a girl to the drive-in movie, then to the malt shop afterward. Everything Jack knew about dating, he had learned from watching *Happy Days*. Fucking, on the other hand—Jack had learned everything he knew about fucking from being a drug-addled, derelict, degenerate piece of shit who hung out at places like the Mecca. As a matter of fact, Jack knew so much about the nastiest kinds of fucking that he knew he could get a five-dollar blow job at the Mecca Theater from a woman with four teeth that night.

He seriously considered heading down to the Mecca right then to get a five-dollar movie ticket and a five-dollar blowjob, but he realized having ten fewer dollars would seriously damage the Dolores date fund, so he just took care of himself. At least he'd made time to watch *Happy Days* when he was a kid or he'd really have been out of his element.

Without *Happy Days*, Jack's vision of a date would be a quick trip over to his dealer's house to suck on the big glass dick, then over to the Ol' Lonesome tavern for a twenty-course meal of one-dollar beers. The girls Jack usually had sex with not only considered that a more than generous use of his money, but also a classy night out, and certainly enough to seal the deal at the end of the night. What was even sadder was that Jack himself had just recently realized why, for normal girls, that did not count as a classy night out.

Jack polished his one pair of Doc Marten boots and tried to make a perfect crease in the cuff of his Levi's by laying several books on them. He didn't have an iron, so he had to be creative. He kept looking for an iron while he was dumpster diving, but had not come across one.

During the three days before his date with Dolores, Jack spent practically every spare moment either planning or thinking about it.

One thing he didn't want to do was go to the coffee shop. It seemed awkward to go in there in the days leading up to the date. "I mean, what was I gonna to say, I can't wait 'til I see you on that date we planned, you remember don't you. That seems a little desperate, even for me." Of course, she remembered the date, and Jack didn't feel like either one of them deserved the additional clumsy conversation that would be the inevitable result of going in there every day.

Plus, he now lacked coffee money, since he was blowing it all on the date. Jack figured she would notice that he wasn't coming in for his normal daily coffee. He assumed she wouldn't think it was strange since they'd just made a serious alteration to their current relationship by agreeing to go on the date at all. On the morning of the date, he planned on showing up for his morning coffee and talking freely about the date. That way, she wouldn't have to wait all day for his confirmation call. For a moment, cold blood ran though Jack's veins when he realized that if the date went poorly, he'd have to find a new place to get coffee. It went away when he realized that anywhere else he went for coffee would cost him about half of what it did at Grounds for Coffee. A silver lining: He'd have to walk further, but he'd save a lot of money in the long run.

In the meantime, he'd been soliciting advice from every person at his disposal, which in totality amounted to very few people. That being the case, Jack decided to widen his pool of advisors. Nearly any living adult had more experience at dating than Jack, so he just started asking people at random, or semi-random.

Stu was the maintenance guy at his building, and he looked like he'd taken a few girls to nice restaurants, so Jack asked him. Todd didn't date much, but he had, somehow along the way, picked up some practical dating tips. Jack even went so far as to ask the guys that dumpster dived his garbage bins. It took some prodding, but Jack discovered that even the dumpster divers had been on a few dates of their own. He still didn't like that they dived the dumpsters that Jack coveted, but they did tell him what they knew about dating.

To the best of his understanding, stemming from this diverse panel of advisors, it appeared that it was not necessary to take a girl to the nicest restaurant in the city for a first date. That much was a relief to Jack. That was exactly what he'd planned to do. It was widely agreed upon by his advisors that he had better spring for a taxi to get around. That one didn't seem negotiable. No car was fine with most girls, especially if you were a city dweller. Lots of people in the city didn't have cars, but that was no excuse to make a girl ride the bus on a first date. For some reason, it appeared that New York City was the only place in America that public transportation was a viable option for car-impaired daters. Jack wished he was a New Yorker for a moment, then realized that getting a taxi once for a date was easier than dealing with a lifetime of smelly, rat-infested subways. Anyhow, it was a problem that might very well remedy itself, seeing as how Dolores had a car of her own and probably preferred driving to riding in a cab anyhow, but Jack had to feel it out.

The next phase of the date was conduct. It was a good general rule to keep conversation on most first dates somewhat light, best to steer clear of possible sore subjects. Molestation, politics, animal rights, abortion, prostitution as a sensible employment option for academically challenged men and women. These were all subjects that Jack figured were possible sore subjects, and best to be avoided altogether.

First dates were all about finding enough common ground that two people decided they were lonely enough to have sex with each other. A relationship might or might not blossom from that first hookup, and if it did, that was the time to find out you hated each other, not before. After that first date with Dolores, Jack really thought he would have dating and relationships figured out.

"It's probably only gonna take 'bout a week for two people to get to know each other. By the time that happens there's a pretty good chance they're gonna hate each other. Or they're gonna dislike each other enough to not want to sleep with each other. Basically, two people have less than a week to have sex, or it probably ain't gonna happen, so they better find a few things they like 'bout each other as soon as possible so that they can start fuckin' immediately. That's how you build a solid fuckin' relationship. Also, if you move in together right away, it's even harder to break up, so you can hate each other even more and still stay together. That's a fuckin' great deal for everyone involved."

Jack was a brave street philosopher. He knew things inherently that others didn't, and he said things that others wouldn't. Jack's learned philosophy that dating was just the pretext and camouflage for fucking was one such example. Nobody says it, but it's what most people are thinking. Or it is what most guys are thinking, at least, and as far as Jack was concerned, the girls should be notified of that fact if they hadn't been already. "It's not cool to keep it a secret, eyes wide open, right."

Before he had dated, he had known how to find girls that understood how it worked. After he dated, he realized that not every girl knew how it worked, and he could never understand how so many of them could have missed such an obvious fact. "How is it that mentally ill, dope fiend prostitutes understand that fuckin' is the lynchpin of human interaction, but professional girls with college degrees think it's mutual admiration. God, them bitches is dumb! I guess there's some shit you just don't learn in a book." To Jack, it seemed like pulling the curtain back on something, but in reverse.

Strangely enough, with the smart girls, steering the conversation as far away from the issue of sex as possible was typically Jack's only chance of getting laid. Not talking about it somehow gave it power. The sexual tension it created masked itself as a meaningful connection, and once that threshold requirement had been met, even the smart girls started inviting him up to their apartments. Whether the smart girls realized it or not, Jack simply found a different route for making sex the primary concern on a date.

Later, and for a very brief period of time, Jack was even able to frame his indigency as a bohemian and artistic lifestyle choice, repudiating conformed and assimilated America in favor of a more evolved existence focused on the realization of the self. Jack found a book in the garbage one time that gave him some stellar talking points. He got more ass from smart rich girls with good jobs during a four-month period, after he put all the pieces together, than he got for the remainder of his life combined.

All that was the master class. Planning one date with Dolores was the survey level. Jack's research revealed that it was proper to attempt a peck on the lips at the completion of a successful first date. A successful date included a minimum of weird, awkward pauses, at least two locations i.e., a restaurant and a movie, and a good flow of light conversation that in no way pertained to sex. On that basis, you could expect a positive response to the peck on the lips. "At that point, you will know if you're bein' prompted for somethin' more simply by how her body moves in your arms. If she melts in your arms all smooth like black tar heroin over a flame, you're in. If she's brittle, like puttin a razor through a choppy rock of angel dust, your night is over, my friend."

Jack still didn't know it all right at that moment. Stu the maintenance guy, who Jack added to his list of advisors when he started planning his date with Dolores, provided him with some nuggets of wisdom:

"Look, I go out with bitches all the time, and some of the time I can't match the phone number in my wallet to no face. I gets a lot of digits. But if I gets the digits, I wanted to hit it enough to gets the digits in the first place, and I be trustin' my own good judgment, ya know. I try to write somethin' down next to their name to help me remember 'em, and hopefully to remember what they likes to eat, o' where they likes to go out. That way when I calls 'em, I say somethin' like ha lets go here o' there, o' let's eat here o' there. And, also, when my wife finds them digits in my pockets, I can just tell her it's some ol' lady who lives in the building who I took out to lunch on her eightieth birthday, o' cos she's got no family, o' some other bullshit. But what I'm getting' at is just this. Women want to think that the guyz they goes out with cares enough 'bout them to, ya know, know what they like, even when we just met them at the club o' something. O', that, at the very least we want them to have fun, and that we care 'bout where they want to go o' whatever, whether we do o' don't.

"So, plannin' a date is the easies' thing in the world. Decide on somethin' that you won't hate doin', and someplace to eat you won't hate eatin'. Then ask, if that's okay with her, and that if she prefers, she can choose the restaurant, o' whatever else you got goin' on. Easy, like that. Trust me, I date several times a week, and I got a wife. Ya know wot I'm saying?"

All adulterous and misogynist motives aside, what

Stu had to say made lots of sense to Jack, and it made planning the date much easier. Going on a date was all about entertaining the person you were going out with. Dating was like everything else in the world: just a means to get what you wanted from somebody.

For once, satisfying his own physical urges wasn't what he had in mind. That was not to say that his aim was entirely altruistic. You could say that Jack's aim was more sinister than using somebody for sex. It was his intention to use this girl for her emotional and mental stability. Jack's was clearly nonexistent and always had been. She worked at a coffee shop, likely for not much more than minimum wage, and probably made no more than twenty bucks in tips a day, but she went to college, maintained an automobile, and had an apartment. It was not Jack's intention to make himself happy at her expense, but if his emotional and mental security had to come at a negative cost to hers, he was willing to make her suffer a little.

Chapter 12

And back to this again. Jack was sure he was shrinking. Somewhere he'd heard that you only stayed your maximum height for seven to ten years, and since he hadn't grown since he was sixteen, he was overdue to start shrinking. Statistics be damned, Jack still felt like he was too young to get short. Maybe he wasn't shrinking, but some asshole had put that seven-to-ten-years statistic out there and Jack had freaked. He wasn't even short. Jack was six-foot-one. At least, he was when he stood up straight, which he almost always did after hearing that shrinking statistic.

Jack couldn't understand why people said things like that, why they didn't just keep their big fat mouths shut. From that time forward, Jack, who was not shrinking, had walked around standing up so straight he had looked like someone had shoved a sign post straight up his butt. The end result was that, because of his hypersensitivity to height and his new overly-erect posture, he now looked taller and crazier. "Man, I fuckin' hate the person who made up statistics. What a fuckin' prick. Why do they have to study things? Why can't we all just be stupid and think we're tall? At least we'd probably be happy."

Sometimes, Jack thought the hardwood floors in Dolores's apartment were making him shorter, and he knew for a fact that lifting heavy things was making him shorter. One day, Dolores asked Jack to lift up the corner of the couch so that she could adjust the rug and Jack blurted out "no fuckin' way" with such apprehension that she was sure he'd misunderstood the question. She repeated the question and received an identical response. She asked why, but Jack couldn't bring himself to tell her: "It's because liftin' shit compresses your vertebrae, and it makes you shorter. If I'm gonna fuckin' shrink, it better be for a good reason, not liftin' some couch." This much should have been clear to anyone: Jack was addicted to being paranoid.

To Jack, moving in together seemed like the next smart thing to do. Moving in was good for staying together because once everybody was moved in it was harder to just leave. Also, back then, it was just how relationships were done. You met each other, went out a few times, fucked a few times, had a pregnancy scare, and then, since you were already sort of making plans to move in, you just shacked up. Dolores had just done her first morning-after pill, and she was sick to her stomach for two days. Jack couldn't handle a child, and he knew it. They'd never know if there had even been a baby to worry about anyway in the first place, but Jack knew it didn't sit right with Dolores.

Dolores came from lonely circumstances herself. She was an only child, and her parents had split when she was a teenager. Her relationship with her mom was poor, and her relationship with her father was nonexistent. After that, Jack had always gotten the feeling that she'd actually wanted to be pregnant that time. Or not that she really wanted to be pregnant, but that she'd have welcomed some stability in the way of a child. Jack had latched onto her because of what he perceived as her stability, but she really only looked stable to Jack because Jack was so unstable that anyone that was not currently committed to an institution looked stable to him. Even though she'd never get pregnant on purpose, Jack was sure that, if it were solely up to her, and she was in fact pregnant, she'd have had the baby.

Abortion was never an option for Dolores. It wasn't a political thing. She was pro-choice, but she'd been clear that she herself would never get an abortion. For Jack, telling Dolores about the brand-new morning-after pill made it possible to erase the mistake of the previous night. It was abortion lite, if you will, and it was easy enough to convince Dolores to take a pill. It was simple to get a prescription from her doctor and make it physically go away. Making it go away emotionally was a harder slog. What men never took into consideration was that even a possible pregnancy was a big deal to a lot of women. The emotional scars took a lot longer to heal for them, and there was usually resentment directed toward the man in the situation. She never openly showed the resentment, but some things were easy enough to figure out even if no one said them out loud.

Would having a child have made things better? Jack didn't know, but probably not. Things would have been different, but life was already complicated enough without that to worry about. Afterward, they settled into a normal sort of living arrangement.

Dolores's apartment was comfortable, and a radical change from the Winthrop. A one-bedroom in a renovated twenties brick building, it was comfortable and had style. There were even framed posters lining the hallways, noting some of the more important events, movies, or industries of the twenties. The posters were all originals, or at least that's what Jack liked to tell visitors, though in reality, they had to have been well-crafted reproductions of originals. Strange plants also littered the areas near the elevators, and there was a check-in window attached to what had used to be the manager's office just inside the front entrance. Jack told people the building was retro art deco, but Jack didn't really know what that meant. It did sound like what he thought the building was, and nobody ever corrected him, which emboldened his continued use of the phrase.

The elevators had those collapsible pull-across gates. Jack figured they were made out of iron, but were painted a gold color, a gold that had worn or chipped off much of the surface of those gates. The sound of those gates opening or closing caused an ear-piercing screech. It really completed the mood. That is, it would have, if Jack had any idea what a retro art deco mood was supposed to feel like. Walking into those elevators felt like walking straight into an early Joan Crawford movie.

Another noisy feature of Dolores's building was the furnace, which came on sporadically at best. In the summer it would come on all day long. It put out so much heat in the summer that you could see distortions in the steam. They reminded Jack of the distortions you see coming off gasoline when you're filling up your gas tank or off hot concrete. Conversely, in the winter, you could go an entire evening without the telltale clanking that let you know a minimal amount of heat was on its way to your apartment. At those times, during those twenty-five-degree nights, Jack would have killed for the opportunity to try to sleep through the sound of metal grinding on other metal that the furnace made when it ran. Waiting for it to kick on in the winter was just as futile as waiting for it to kick off in the summer. That summer, Jack would sit, soaked in sweat, trying to enjoy his favorite soap opera, *General Hospital.* Meanwhile, that winter he would have killed to see just a hint of that heat distortion that indicated that the furnace was on. All of this was happening on top of Jack's shrinking; or maybe, he postulated, it was the heat melting him. Multiple daily measurements to ensure his six-foot-one status were not only common but an activity religiously performed. It was all becoming too much, and Jack was getting ready to snap again.

Considering the faulty premise on which Dolores and Jack's relationship was based, it lasted for much longer than one might have expected. Not only that, but they were actually quite content being with one another a good deal of the time. Jack loved Dolores, but more as a caretaker that he was allowed to fuck from time to time. Dolores loved Jack, but more like a beloved classic car that could never do anything but sit in a garage and deteriorate.

They made it work for better than a year, though, and during that time Jack reached the pinnacle of his success as a functioning human being. Dolores was a high point for him, even if it was destined to failure from the start. "Hey, some people never even got a month of stability, much less a year."

The ritualistic swallowing of Jack's Depakote started and ended every one of his days. Just another of his structure-building activities in a regimen of structure-building activities designed to give his life order. Popping that Depakote was an important one, though. Unlike every medication Jack had ever been on, the Depakote worked. Originally, it was developed for epilepsy, and it was an effective anti-seizure medication. Somewhere along the way, somebody figured out that people using the Depakote who also had bipolar disorder were doing a lot better with their mood swings.

As disorganized and scattered as Jack's life had been, it was ironic that everything about his it boiled down to a ritual. Before the first card was dealt, or drink taken, before the needle hit the vein, or even before the ritualistic closing of the locking door in the mental ward, there was the ritual itself. In his mind, he asked forgiveness for what he'd done, and especially what he was about to do. And, of course, he sought forgiveness for crashing and burning that night, or morning, or year, or whatever the case turned out to be. It was the rare occasion that Jack gave any thought as to who or what the ritualistic plea for forgiveness was directed at, but he always went through with it, hoping there was something looking out for him. During that time, Jack started paying a lot more attention to where these pleas might be going, almost as much attention as he'd give to the content of these pleas themselves. Still, for all he knew, they just floated off the top of his head and into the cloudy northwest atmosphere that was always residing right above his head. But at least what happened to them concerned him, and Jack could only call that progress.

The content of these ritual conversations was now unknown. As Jack stared that morning's Depakote in the face, he asked that it continue to give him stability of mind, so that he could use his energy to try to create a good life for Dolores and himself. Even though he'd given her full disclosure of his past in his own words, she really couldn't understand. She was not prone to those mental quirks and physical addictions. For a lot of people, it was hard to feel empathy for someone's plight unless that person had lived through similar experiences, or at least could apply the feeling of a difficult experience to another's plight. It was not that people were all sociopaths—most really want to be empathic across a broad spectrum—but without firsthand experience, it was hard. Jack was no different. He had a hard time understanding the pain of others unless he'd felt something similar under similar circumstances. He sensed that Dolores wanted to be empathetic, but she couldn't really get it because she hadn't lived it.

Even the greatest storyteller could still only tell a story. Some stories could only fall on deaf ears; some things could only be experienced. Painful and powerful experiences could usually only have a limited audience because of their personal nature. That Dolores had not endured these things made Jack thankful, because he loved her, but because she had not lived these experiences, he knew they could never connect on the level required to truly understand each other and be happy. That's what Jack figured whenever he unloaded some sordid detail of his past on Dolores. "But what the fuck do I know. I'm a fucked-up, degenerate, loser, the biggest in the world, so far as I can tell."

But for a while, he pulled the wool over everybody's eyes. Even Laurence started to believe Jack might have clawed his way out of the addicted underbelly of society.

On moving day, Laurence was on inspector duty, like always. When he called Jack, it was the first time they'd spoken since their mom's funeral. Laurence may have been disappointed, disgusted, or disgruntled, but one way or the other he'd kept good tabs on Jack. He had made sure he knew Jack's phone number and address. Jack, of course, had made no such effort to keep track of Laurence. Jack had figured Laurence felt obligated to continue to be the big brother. It was what their mom would've wanted, and they both knew it. Looking after Jack, even if it was from behind the scenes, was Laurence's birthright, and he would fulfill it despite anyone's, including Jack's, objections.

Moving day was Laurence's opportunity to assume his big brother role in the largest way possible, and as noted, neither Jack, nor Dolores, nor Christ himself was going to stand in his way. Jack did need Laurence's help moving, but he did not need the constant, condescending commentary that Laurence also considered to be his birthright and responsibility, and Jack knew it was coming the moment Laurence set foot into that apartment.

Jack, for a moment, actually wondered if Laurence had tapped his phone. The phone was the only place he could recall having talked about moving with anyone. Maybe Todd had told him; maybe Todd gave him my phone number; maybe Todd had been a double agent the entire time. Jack didn't really know. Whatever the truth, the fact remained that when Laurence called one day he knew precisely when Dolores and Jack planned to move, and he showed up to help without Jack ever contacting him whatsoever.

Jack thought that if he and Dolores had never moved, he could have avoided seeing Laurence indefinitely. If he showed up for moving day, Jack figured he would definitely show up for a medical emergency, and Jack decided right then and there that he would have to make sure to never become physically ill again. Being sick was bad enough, but if it meant Laurence would be there, that was so much incentive to stay healthy. Maybe, Jack thought, if they'd stayed put, Laurence never would have called. If he never called, he probably wouldn't have shown up to help them move and criticize everything they had, everything they did, and every way they did it. Similar to a medical emergency, Jack decided that if Laurence was going to show up whenever he moved, that he'd just make sure never to move again. If that kept Laurence away, it was well worth it.

But maybe he would have come out of the woodwork eventually anyhow. And then he would have criticized the woodwork, and complained about the way Jack was moving the woodwork. But he never really had a chance. Dolores wanted a dog, and a garden, and more space than her little one-bedroom apartment afforded them. And Jack wanted to give her all of those things more than anything else. Operating on a selfless plane was not native to Jack, but he thought it felt good.

The phone rang. *Must be fuckin' Laurence*, Jack

thought. "Even his ring looks down on me."

"Hello," Jack said.

"So, are you ready to go?"

That was his impolite way of asking Jack to come downstairs to let him in. Without him saying so, Jack already knew that he was talking to him on his cell phone outside the building. He was just waiting for Jack to ask where he was, so that he could say, "Well, I'm standing outside your building ready to move all your crap. Where are you?" Jack wasn't going to give him the pleasure, so he just said:

"Okay, be right down."

"Yeah, okay," Laurence said.

The other pleasure Jack would deprive him of today would be the opportunity to silently judge Dolores. Since Laurence and Todd would both be there to help him, it didn't make sense that Dolores should be there. Since there were three of them to handle the heavy stuff, Jack told her to go have fun with her friends for the day, and that she and Jack would get the light stuff the next day. "And I knew I was goin to shrink like a whole inch on movin day." Dolores didn't have many friends, and the ones she did have she didn't spend a great deal of time with, so Jack was sure it seemed like an odd request. But she was sweet, and so she just said "okay." That way, she wouldn't have to endure meeting and subsequently spending the day with

Laurence. A whole day was a lot of Laurence to handle for anybody, even Jack, but at least the long years of his life preceding that day had conditioned him for it. Dolores had no such conditioning to fall back on. There really was no good reason Jack could think of for Dolores to meet Laurence. Laurence was more than capable of making a judgment about somebody he'd never met by simply looking at the photographs and belongings that were all over their apartment. How did two people born from the same gene pool turn out so different? They were born to the same parents. They'd die with the same family name on their respective headstones. But nothing else about them resembled one another in the least. Jack wondered a lot about how that happened. He had never come up with a satisfactory answer, but he assumed their parents would want them to stick together to the greatest extent possible. That was never going to happen, but Jack did begrudgingly make infrequent attempts to tolerate Laurence's presence. He figured moving day ought to satisfy that minimal effort quotient for at least a year or two.

Right around the time that Laurence and Jack had gotten the bed and dressers into the moving van, he started to wonder where the rest of their help was.

The phone rang. *Fuckin' Todd, not showin' up*, Jack thought. "Even his ring feels like he's going to leave me hangin'."

"Ha, dude, I'm way stoned, and I sort of don't want to really see your brother either," Todd said.

"Is that right! Well, that makes two of us, but Laurence won't mind. Laurence never gets sick of his own company. He may not even notice that you didn't show up. By the way, how did Laurence know I was movin' today?"

"Sorry man, I totally gotta go. Later."

At first, Jack was kind of pissed. And, for a moment, he envisioned going over to Todd's place and catching him sleeping off that stone and smacking him in the head with his bong. But, right about then, Jack actually understood his point of view, and if Jack were him, he'd want to sit on his couch and get stoned rather than see Jack's brother, too. And why did Jack want him there anyway? Basically, Jack wanted Todd there so that he didn't have to talk to Laurence himself.

A few minutes later, Dolores walked into the apartment with bags full of meatball subs from MSM Deli on Sixth Avenue. Jack silently wished she had walked in five minutes earlier. If Todd had known they had meatball subs from MSM, he probably would have showed up. People remember the oddest things. One of the only things that Laurence and Jack could unequivocally agree on was that MSM meatball subs were the best meal that could be had for less than ten bucks. And that the sandwiches had to consist only of meatballs, sauce, and cheese. Of course, that was exactly what was on these subs, which were both plentiful and numerous. On the weight of one sentence that Jack had mumbled a few months back that went something like, "Me and my brother love those meatball subs at that place, just meatballs, cheese, and sauce," she'd taken it upon herself to provide Laurence and Jack with their favorite meal for lunch, and in the process, leave Laurence with an impression that would be hard to criticize, even for him.

How could you not be in love with a girl that went out of her way to impress your pretentious brother after she'd been cut loose for the day? And Laurence couldn't help but be impressed. Jack didn't even tell Laurence how she knew about the sandwiches. Jack just let him ponder whether she had great intuition, insider information, or uncannily good taste. Laurence ate his sub with a slightly amused, slightly confused, but completely content look on his face. For about three seconds, Jack saw something he had used to like about Laurence, something that hadn't happened since they were younger. It reminded Jack of when Laurence had first gotten his driver's license and a part-time job. He'd taken Jack to MSM for meatball subs, and then they had gone to a movie and eaten candy and drank pop until they were nauseous. The feeling only lasted for three seconds, no more. Jack counted. But still, it was nice to see that it was in there somewhere. With an ever-diminishing list of reasons for them to stay in contact, Dolores had given them a reason to stay brothers for at least one more day.

Puyallup was a small town outside of Tacoma. Actually, it was a large town. Actually, it was a small city. That was what they called it, anyway. The downtown was filled with turn-of-the-century buildings, and the houses in the old part of town also dated back to that time. Main Street was actually called Main Street. The fact that a railroad ran through town was still a big deal to the citizens, but the annual fair, which took place on fairgrounds that had once housed an internment camp for Japanese citizens during World War II, was its main attraction. Puyallup was a town that was actually a city that was nostalgic about being a town. It even had its own little fire department, and twelve police officers. Was this the municipal apparatus of a town or a city? Who knew.

Puyallup was where Jack and Dolores's new place was. Everything about that city, or town, or what-ever, was small, and so was everything about Jack and Dolores's life there. They lived in the littlest house, with the littlest yard, on the littlest street in that little city. And inside the front door of that littlest house lived two people with the littlest lives in that little city—for the time being, anyway. How it was that their new two-bedroom house along with front and back yard could possibly be smaller than Dolores's little one-bedroom apartment was beyond Jack. But they had a yard, and a yard was important to Dolores.

Afterword

I can't say where you came across this book, but my best guess would be that you found it in a box of castoff garbage by the curb outside the cheap apartment complex at the end of your road. That guy that lived in the noisy apartment was just evicted, and this little novella was just some superfluous stack of somewhat uninformative paper disguised as a book by a cheap book binding and publishing house logo. Trust me, even the publishing house logo is a smoke show, just my plausible camouflage for a self-publishing operation consisting of me, and me alone, a one-man band.

As you might have already guessed from the title, this is the first part of a story. Specifically, it's the story of Jack, a guy that consistently failed to clear a bar so low he could have tripped over it. Jacks are all over the world. Most of you know a Jack. I've known several. I've even been a Jack in the past. I spend a lot of time and effort these days doing my best not to turn back into a Jack, but I digress. That noisy guy from the recently vacated apartment is definitely a Jack. He's not a bad guy. He's actually a pretty fun guy under the right set of circumstances. Anyway, there are two more novellas, and Jack has got a lot more story to tell.

Next up is *Courting Mediocrity*, and that's exactly what Jack does. If you dig through enough dump-sters, you might find a copy. If not, your best bet is probably the free book rack outside the Powell's in downtown Portland. Hey, at least it won't cost you any money!

About the Author

I was a homeless teenager. Now I own a home. I was a high school dropout. Now I'm an attorney. I was an alcoholic. Now I'm sober. I was a kid well into adulthood. Now I'm the adult parent of kids. I was alone. Now I have people. I was a punk rock teenager. Now I'm a punk rock middleager. I was Jack. Now I'm Chris.

Thank you for reading Sleeping in the Daytime. I hope you enjoyed it. Reviews are the single most important factor to the success or failure of a book. Please take a moment and leave a short review at one, or preferably both of the links below. Also please connect with me on social media, and join my email list for freebies.

Connect with Me and Subscribe to the Email List

https://blandcoffeepublishing.com

Also by Christopher J. Stockwell

If you love slummin' it in the PNW, check out the rest of the down and out series, my first gritty novel *The Antagonist's Handbook*, and the two books of the *City Attorney's Office* series. If you don't feel icky afterward, we'll refund your money.

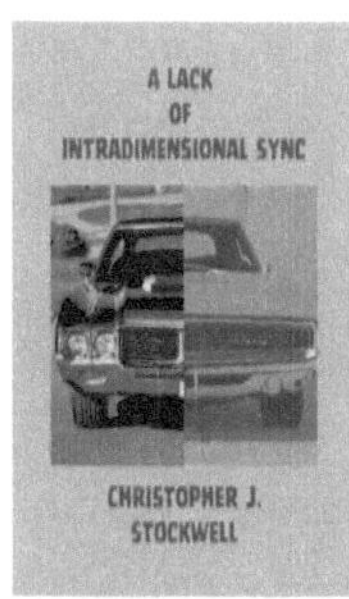

A Lack of Intradimensional Sync
Jon is everywhere an nowhere. He slips out of himself and rides the infinite roads of existence itself. But infinite time is eventually infinite torment for a human brain that never asked for anything more than normality. Expected Release 2026.

Down and Out in Seattle and Tacoma Novella Two: Courting Mediocrity
See what's next for Jack. Quiet anonymity in a boring town or city or whatever isn't his style. Debauchery, Deterioration, and Degeneration are.

Down and Out in Seattle and Tacoma Novella Three: Squatting in the Shadow of an Ant
Prisons, institutions, and punk houses! See how Jack winds up. Is that a light at the end of the tunnel? Yes, it is a car intent on running poor Jack down.

The Complete Down and Out in Seattle and Tacoma Series
The three novellas of the Down and Out in Seattle and Tacoma Series in one volume. The down and out novellas are like coke, alcohol, and cigarettes. You can enjoy them separately, but they were meant to be consumed together.

City Attorney's Office Book One: Professional Camouflage
This first of a series of short romance novels is nothing more than a thinly-veiled disguise for a social and political satire piece. Is is dark humor, literary existential bullshit, a boring workplace romance. I don't fuckin' know, and I wrote the book.

City Attorney's Office Book Two: The Land of Lollipops and Suckers
This second, and last (?) of the City Attorney's Office books. People always ask me if a lawyer's life is like Law & Order or the Good Wife. It's neither, it's mostly like Matlock and Perry Mason having a beer with Saul Goodman. Enjoy!

The Complete City Attorney's Office Series

If you liked the love triangle between Ben, Maria, and Erin, you'll get closure. If you liked that fact that Ben is a monkey wrench dismantling the necessary cogs of justice, it's in there as well. If you just want the series to be over, so do it. Your welcome!

The Antagonist's Handbook

Stockwell's first novel, written under the pseudonym Christopher J. Heassler details the emergence of a paparazzi gang who exploit celebrities. The Antagonist's Handbook has long been out of print, but is scheduled for re-release in 2026.

www.ingramcontent.com/pod-product-compliance
Lightning Source LLC
Chambersburg PA
CBHW031056310726
48969CB00007B/2295